OUT OF
TUNE

OUT OF TUNE

NORAH McCLINTOCK

ORCA BOOK PUBLISHERS

Library and Archives Canada Cataloguing in Publication

McClintock, Norah, author
Out of tune / Norah McClintock.
(Riley Donovan)

Issued also in print and electronic formats.
ISBN 978-1-4598-1465-3 (pbk.).—ISBN 978-1-4598-1466-0 (pdf).—
ISBN 978-1-4598-1467-7 (epub)

I. Title. II. Series: McClintock, Norah. Riley Donovan
PS8575.C620925 2017   jC813'.54   C2017-900856-0
                    C2017-900857-9

First published in the United States, 2017
Library of Congress Control Number: 2017933015

Summary: In the third Riley Donovan mystery for teen readers, Riley tries
to figure out who killed a young musical prodigy.

RECYCLED
Paper made from
recycled material
FSC® C103567
FSC
www.fsc.org

Orca Book Publishers is dedicated to preserving the environment and has
printed this book on Forest Stewardship Council® certified paper.

Orca Book Publishers gratefully acknowledges the support for
its publishing programs provided by the following agencies:
the Government of Canada through the Canada Book Fund and the
Canada Council for the Arts, and the Province of British Columbia
through the BC Arts Council and the Book Publishing Tax Credit.

Cover design by Jenn Playford
Cover photography by Getty Images

ORCA BOOK PUBLISHERS
www.orcabook.com

Printed and bound in Canada.

20   19   18   17   •   4   3   2   1

Also by Norah McClintock

Taken (2009)
She Said, She Saw (2011)
Guilty (2012)
I, Witness (2012)
About That Night (2014)
Tru Detective (2015)
Trial by Fire (2016)
From Above (2016)

ONE

I first got involved on the Saturday following the Wednesday that was officially "the last time anyone saw the missing girl." I got involved because of Charlie.

It was a clear mid-autumn afternoon. Around Moorebridge, where I live, that means field after brown field cleared and prepped for winter. It also means vast expanses of crimson, lemon, umber, pumpkin and tangerine in the tree breaks between fields and in the woodlots and forest that surround the town. We were on a road that hugged the perimeter of a stretch of forest north of town, we being Charlie, Ashleigh and, of course, me.

"You can't be serious." The aggrieved expression on Ashleigh's face was a perfect match for her whiny tone of voice. She'd been complaining more or less all morning, which was starting to drive me crazy, and Charlie looked ready to strangle her. "What would she be doing way out here?"

Charlie spoke through gritted teeth. "Someone might have seen her. They might have seen if she was with someone."

"At the Trading Post?" Ashleigh shook her head impatiently.

"It's possible," Charlie said.

"And the Pines—which, may I point out, closed for the season two weeks ago? Or Broom's Corners, population fifty-three. Unless someone died recently."

"You can always turn back," Charlie said. If I had to bet, I'd bet he was hoping she would.

She didn't. "Tell me again why we're doing all this," she said instead.

"You know why we're doing it." Charlie is generally a Clark Kent type. Mild mannered. Even gentle. But not at that exact moment. He spoke slowly, through clenched teeth, as if he was trying to tamp down the exasperation that had been evident from the first moment Ashleigh decided to join us on our outing. "We're doing it because Alicia is missing."

We had been out on our bikes all morning, delivering *Have You Seen This Girl?* flyers around town, and now we were heading out of town.

"But it's a long way to Broom's Corners," Ashleigh said, "and there's zero chance that Alicia would ever go there."

Charlie's jaw clenched.

"If you want to wait here," I said quickly, "I'll go with Charlie and you can take a break." Anything to restore the peace between the two of them or, at least, cut down on Ashleigh's incessant grumbling.

"No, no, I'll come." She said this with a heavy sigh, as if she were doing us a huge favor.

Charlie glanced at me, rolling his eyes. All I could do was shrug helplessly and hope that Ashleigh's mood would improve.

We rode roughly two miles along a tree-lined, two-lane blacktop until we reached the tiny hamlet of Broom's Corners. It consisted of a dozen or so houses spread out along the east-west and north-south crossroads. It also had a gas station (the vacant-eyed guy at the cash register barely looked at the photo on the flyer), an antiques store that sold mostly old farm furniture and knickknacks from estate sales and wood from old torn-down barns and farm sheds, an agricultural-implements dealership (the sharply dressed salesman promised to put the poster up right in the showroom) and a bakery, where the two women behind the counter, one old, one young with a small child clinging to her, studied the flyer with concern. A dental office and a real estate office flanked a burger place in the smallest strip mall I have ever seen. We papered tiny Broom's Corners with flyers.

From there we rode back on a different road that ran beside the farthest edge of a large wooded area that bordered Moorebridge to the north.

"Are we going home?" Ashleigh asked, her voice buoyed with hope.

"Not yet."

Instead we rode about a mile to the Trading Post, which consisted of the Trading Post itself and its burger shack, where you could buy burgers, hot dogs, fries and onion rings and eat them at the picnic tables on the adjacent lawn. Across the parking lot was a laundromat that was heavily used by campers, RVers, tourists and truckers. Charlie pulled some flyers out from under the brick in the milk crate attached to the back of his bike and handed a couple to each of us. "Laundromat," he said to Ashleigh. To me, "Utility posts. I'll do the Trading Post."

Ashleigh scowled at the face on the flyer. "What does that even mean—*missing*? So she's not home. Big deal. She's sixteen. She has free will. Maybe she even developed a spine. She could be anywhere."

"Developed a spine?" I knew from Ashleigh's body language, comments and general lack of enthusiasm that she was not as concerned about the possibility of missing Alicia Allen as Charlie was.

"She sucks up to everyone," Ashleigh said. "There are two reasons people do that, Riley. To manipulate. Or to please, in order to be loved. Alicia is definitely the latter. She's one of those girls you just want to kill. Little Miss Perfect. Since kindergarten, no less. Teacher's pet since then too."

"Wait a minute," I said. "What was she doing in your kindergarten class? She's older than you. She's graduating this year, isn't she?"

"We had a joint junior-senior kindergarten class," Charlie said.

"Then, of course, Miss Perfect skipped a grade or two," Ashleigh added. "Not that it's at all relevant to my point."

"Which is?" I asked.

"Which is that there were four parts to the show."

"The one in kindergarten?" I asked.

"That's what I said, isn't it? There were two musical numbers and two skits. Our class spent a whole month rehearsing for a show for our families. Everyone was supposed to have the chance to participate. But guess who was in all four parts?" Ashleigh's face turned red with remembered resentment.

"Come on, you're not still upset about that, are you?" Charlie shook his head in disbelief. "Ms. Farmington, our teacher, didn't realize until nearly performance day that Ashleigh didn't have a part," he explained. "You could have spoken up, Ashleigh. You could have told her."

"I was five years old! And anyway, what does that have to do with Alicia getting four parts?" A spray of spit filled the air between them. This was turning into a serious argument.

"Whoa, you two. Time-out," I said.

"No one has heard from Alicia in over two days." Charlie directed this to me, as if he needed to justify himself. "She's not answering her phone. Her parents are worried sick. They live on our street, Riley. I've known Alicia my whole life." He glowered at Ashleigh. "It's not like I twisted your arm. You volunteered to help."

"I didn't know it would take all day."

"We're almost done," Charlie said. "There's just this place and the Pines."

Ashleigh's eyes bugged out. "The Pines is at least a mile down the road! And it's closed. Why bother?"

"Maybe the caretaker saw her."

"Oh, come on, Charlie. What are the chances?"

"You didn't have to come," Charlie said with barely contained frustration. I didn't think he realized it, but he was crushing the flyers as he curled his hands into fists.

"I have an idea," I said. One that would get me away from the two of them for a little while. "Why don't you two paper this place with flyers and then get a hot chocolate at the Trading Post? I'll ride down to the Pines."

"You don't know how to get there," Charlie said, at the exact same moment that Ashleigh said, "Terrific. Thanks, Riley. I owe you big-time. And don't worry. You can't get lost. You just go down the road that way"—she pointed—"until you get to the big sign that says *The Pines* with the arrow pointing to it." As she said this, she shot Charlie a withering look. "It's not exactly hard to find."

I mounted my bike before Charlie could speak again. "Wait for me here," I called as I pedaled off.

The air was redolent with the slow decay of autumn. The woods on either side of the road were silent. It was a pleasant change from Ashleigh and Charlie's sniping at each other.

I had to agree with Charlie. No one had strong-armed Ashleigh into joining us. Nor had either of us suggested in any way that we would think badly of her if she chose not to come. But that wasn't what had happened. She'd said okay, and then she'd started to grouse. I was glad we were almost done.

The road to the Pines was more uphill than I would have liked, but that meant it would be a down-hill coast back to Charlie and Ashleigh. I'd worked up a sweat by the time I saw the sign with its huge red arrow pointing left, and it was a relief to reach the cabins at the end of the resort's long driveway. I stopped and took a big gulp from my water bottle.

I set my bike on its kickstand and walked toward the cabin with *Office* over the door. I turned the knob and stepped inside. The front counter, which divided the small room in half, was unstaffed. The door behind the desk was ajar, giving me a glimpse of a tidy desk and an old-fashioned beige telephone.

"Hello!" I called.

No answer. I tried again. Louder.

"Hel-lo-oh!"

Still no answer.

I slid a couple of flyers onto the counter, grabbed the pen that was chained down and began to compose a note on the back of an out-of-date *What's Happening In and Around Moorebridge* brochure. A voice behind me made me jump.

"Can I help you with something?"

I spun around. A man in faded denim overalls, a plaid flannel shirt and a plaid hat with the earflaps turned up stood behind me, toolbox in work-gloved hand. He had the ruddy face of someone who spent a lot of time outdoors. His sharp blue eyes went to the counter where I had started to compose my note.

"Oh, hey. My name is Riley. Riley Donovan."

"Gord Cooper." He set his toolbox on the counter and pulled off one glove. We shook. His hand was large and warm and smooth.

"We're handing out these flyers." I gave him one. "A girl is missing. I don't suppose you've seen her, have you?"

He stared at the picture before shaking his head slowly.

"Afraid I haven't seen her. But then we haven't had much traffic down here since we closed for the season. How long has she been missing?"

"Since Wednesday."

Gord Cooper looked at the photo again. "Well, I'll keep my eyes open. But from what I hear, no one comes here this time of year except by accident."

"Well, if you do happen to see her, her parents' number is there."

"Okay."

Before I was ready for it, it was time for my rendez-vous with Charlie and Ashleigh. I found them sitting on the Trading Post's front porch, both clutching large takeout cups of hot chocolate. Mercifully, they weren't squabbling. Unfortunately, this was because they had stopped talking to each other completely. They were faced away from each other, and both were scrolling through their phones. All in all, it was an improvement.

Charlie was the first to look up.

"They're putting together a search party for tomorrow," he said.

Ashleigh managed to show her disapproval without taking her eyes from her own phone. "Her folks should learn to relax."

"It's not her parents who are organizing the search party. It's the cops. A truck driver saw one of these flyers. He thinks he saw Alicia going into the woods. The cops are asking for volunteers. You'll come, right?" He was looking at me.

"Sure," I said.

Charlie didn't ask Ashleigh, and Ashleigh didn't say a word, not then and not any time later in the day, even though we texted back and forth a couple of times. So I was surprised to see her at the muster location first thing the next morning, bleary-eyed and clutching a takeout latte.

TWO

"No offense, but I wasn't expecting you," I said.

Ashleigh's mouth turned down as if she was going to spit.

"Charlie already thinks I'm the Wicked Witch of the West," she said. "And look around. What would happen to my reputation if I *didn't* show up when literally the whole rest of the town did?"

"It's not even figuratively the whole rest of the town," I said, although I had to admit that it was a pretty impressive crowd. "And exactly what reputation are we talking about?"

"I don't want everyone at school to think I hated Alicia or anything. I mean, what if she turns up dead?"

I glanced around hastily. Someone had said Alicia's parents were here, but I had no idea what they looked like. I'd have hated for either of them to over-hear Ashleigh.

"Well, I'm glad you're here," I said. "Let's go and see what we're supposed to do."

We joined the healthy turnout from school, the dozens of worried adults, and the police over at the mustering area. Aunt Ginny was there, of course. She wasn't coordinating the search—the police chief was taking care of that himself—but she was in charge of one of the four volunteer search teams that had been assigned different quadrants of the woods. Each quadrant had been subdivided, and each was under the supervision of a police officer. We, the searchers, were lined up about ten feet from each other and told to walk each quadrant slowly, eyes scanning the ground in front of us. It was the most efficient way to search dense woods.

People had come out because they knew Alicia or her parents. I'd come mostly because of Charlie and because I wanted to help. Although Alicia and I attended the same sprawling regional high school, she was two years ahead of me, which, combined with the fact I was relatively new in town, meant that I knew her only by sight and reputation.

Sight-wise, she was pretty—thick, wavy chestnut hair, large brown eyes, delicate nose, pillowy lips, an easy smile. She had a killer body—long-legged, slim, perky breasts and a butt that was made for the skinny jeans she liked to wear. The kind of girl boys stare at and girls envy.

Reputation-wise, she was known for her talent. Alicia was reportedly destined for a career as a professional—some said virtuoso—violinist. She competed at the national level and had been winning awards since picking up the violin as a preschooler.

She was top-of-the-honor-roll smart, drooled over by practically every male at school, and, seemingly impossible given her attributes, she was reportedly universally liked.

She was also an only child. Mrs. Allen, a retired teacher, had married Mr. Allen, an actuary, relatively late in life. They never expected to have children, so when Mrs. Allen became pregnant, they considered it almost a miracle. They doted on Alicia, who by all accounts was a good daughter and caused her parents only minimal trouble, which they cheerfully put down to growing pains.

Charlie joined us, greeting Ashleigh with an arched eyebrow. She met his eyes evenly and unapologetically. I broke the tension by asking Charlie to point out Alicia's parents.

Mrs. Allen was pear-shaped and wore her gray-streaked hair in a tight halo of curls. She was standing with two other women. None of them were talking. One of them had a hand on Mrs. Allen's arm. Apparently Mr. Allen, who was in his late sixties, had arthritis in one knee that made it painful for him to walk for extended periods of time. Charlie said he was waiting at search headquarters, which was a police van parked at the end of an old logging access road that constituted the mustering area.

A police officer with a megaphone stepped up onto an overturned milk crate. We were about to get under way.

A weird ripple went through the crowd—a sort of collective intake of air combined with a wave of turned heads. And no wonder. A tall bearded man pushed through the volunteers, who gave way wordlessly when they saw what he was carrying—a hunting rifle.

Uniformed cops swarmed the man, pinning his arms and relieving him of his weapon.

"Hey!" the man shouted. "Hey, I just come like everyone else, to look for that girl."

"That's fine, Rafe," one of the officers said. "But you're going to have to do it unarmed, like everyone else."

I turned to Ashleigh and Charlie. Ashleigh rolled her eyes. Charlie was the one who explained, "Town character."

"Town character?" Ashleigh said. "Town nutbar is more like it!"

Rafe turned and glowered at Ashleigh, who cringed and stepped behind me.

Finally, lined up the way we'd been instructed, we started the slow, painstaking search.

Ashleigh walked the line to my immediate left. To my right, Charlie advanced with measured steps, his gaze unwavering from the rough, scrubby terrain, alert to any sign of Alicia or evidence of any human presence. If we spotted, say, a cigarette butt or discarded food wrapper or soda can or anything else, we were to stop and signal our quadrant leader. In our case, that was Detective Josh Martin, one of Aunt Ginny's colleagues. He would make sure that whatever we found was photographed in place, collected and tagged.

"At this point we have no reason to suspect foul play," the police chief told us before we were divided into search teams. "But we won't know anything for sure until we locate Alicia. In the meantime, we're going to be trampling pretty much anything and everything out here, and there will be no going back to a pristine scene if we need to. So I want you to report everything you find, and I do mean every-thing, people. We don't know at this point what, if anything, we may need or what may turn out to be useful. That means we're going to err on the side of caution. Is everyone clear on that?"

Judging by all the nods, everyone was.

So far my team had turned up half a dozen ciga-rette butts, despite the recent lack of precipitation, the layer of dead leaves blanketing the ground and the conspicuous *No Fires* warnings clearly posted all over the area. We had also located two squashed beer cans, an empty cigarette package, a used-up matchbook, an earring (which caused a flurry of excitement until Alicia's mother tearfully declared that it did not belong to Alicia) and a crumpled valentine to Bobby from Melissa, who, judging from her large, loopy, slightly off-balanced letters, couldn't have been more than six years old. Each find brought Detective Martin and a uniformed officer who did the actual photographing, collecting and tagging after Detective Martin had inspected the item.

We had mustered to search the woods because so far Alicia had failed to turn up in any of her usual places—the rehearsal room at school, her violin teacher's house, any of her friends' houses or anywhere else in town where she was known to spend time. Also, rumor had it that a man in a pickup truck had reported seeing someone who matched Alicia's general description heading into the woods late Wednesday afternoon. He wasn't prepared to swear it was Alicia, but the girl he'd seen had shoulder-length chestnut hair like Alicia's, was wearing a dark jacket (Alicia's was navy blue) and carried a reddish backpack (Alicia's was burgundy), so it was definitely worth a thorough look.

"What would she even be doing out here?" Ashleigh asked, glancing at me from my left. "Don't tell me she's a tree hugger or bird lover too."

"Keep your eyes on the ground in front of you," Charlie scolded from my right. "You're supposed to be looking for clues."

Ashleigh rolled her eyes. "I would hardly miss a body if I stumbled across one." In what I can only describe as a cosmic slap of irony, Ashleigh let out a shriek, which caused our whole line to stop and stare. Ashleigh's arms flew up in the air, and she crashed to the ground with another, slightly smaller scream. When I went to help her, I saw Detective Martin making his way toward us.

"What is it?" His eyes were sharp on the ground, searching, as I hauled Ashleigh to her feet. "What did you find?"

Ashleigh's cheeks reddened. "I tripped." She was standing on one foot, clinging to me for support, and now gingerly lowered her other foot to the ground to test it with her weight. "The ground is uneven around here."

"If you keep your eyes on the ground, you should be able to avoid tripping or stumbling," Detective Martin said.

"It was an accident," Ashleigh muttered in my ear. She continued to hang on to me as she limped, somewhat dramatically, if you ask me, the few steps back into line. Detective Martin watched her with unforgiving eyes.

Before he left, he cautioned the rest of our team to watch out for dips and gullies in the land that could cause a person to lose his or her footing. He stared pointedly at Ashleigh.

"If you ask me, searching the woods is a waste of time," Ashleigh muttered once we were moving again.

"She was last seen around here," I reminded her.

"If I was going to take off, it wouldn't be to anywhere around here, that's for sure," Ashleigh said. She had grown up in town, and she often told me she'd had enough of the place to last a lifetime. When Ashleigh dreamed about life after Moorebridge, she thought about places like New York City—urban jungles filled with shopping possibilities. She was planning to move as far away as she could to go to university, and she swore that she was never, ever going to move back. Her parents could count on seeing her at Christmas, but besides that, she said, nothing could ever induce her to spend one moment longer than necessary staring at the same boring faces she'd been looking at since she was born. Nevertheless, she turned her eyes back to the ground and settled into the task at hand. The same couldn't be said for everyone.

Next to Charlie, from closest to farthest, were Carrie Denison, Tina Bell and Desiree Desjardins, a tight trio of seventeen-year-olds. I knew them by sight. I had also gleaned a few clues to their character from the more-or-less constant chatter that Tina was keeping up about the clothes and accessories featured in the latest issue of *InStyle* magazine. Carrie responded, although, if you asked me, her comments lacked enthusiasm or real interest. Her mind was clearly elsewhere, but it wasn't on the search for Alicia, judging by the many, many times she looked up and down and all around—in short, anywhere but directly on the ground in front of her. Desiree spoke the least and only when a question was specifically directed at her, and then always in a hushed tone, as if she was embarrassed by her friends.

Tina's mindless prattle was annoying. Its triviality under the circumstances infuriated me. Surprisingly, it seemed to rankle Ashleigh even more.

"Hey," she called over me to Tina. "If you don't want to search properly, then you shouldn't be here."

Tina shot her a withering look.

Carrie jumped in to defend her friend. "Why don't you mind your own business?"

"At least I'm here because I care," Ashleigh said. "I'm not a hypocrite like you. You don't even like Alicia."

Carrie's face turned red. Tina took up the sword for her.

"*You* didn't even know Alicia," she snarled at Ashleigh. She glanced at me. "Same goes for you. So what are *you* doing here?" I couldn't help noticing her use of the past tense, as if she was assuming the worst.

Ashleigh glowered at me as if it were all my fault for dragging her here, which I didn't do.

Every now and then someone signaled a halt and called for Detective Martin, but that happened less often the deeper we went into the woods.

Eventually Tina let out a dramatic sigh and said, "Please tell me it's almost time for a break."

"I wish," Carrie said. "I feel like we've been out here all day, and it's only nine thirty."

"No it's not. It's nearly eleven," Tina said.

"My watch says nine thirty."

"Who even uses a watch anymore?" Tina's tone was dismissive.

"It was a gift from my grandma."

"Exactly. It's yesterday's technology. The battery probably wore out or something."

"I must have made a mistake when I was trying to set the date," Carrie said. "The instructions don't make any sense. I try to do what they say, and I always end up pressing the wrong buttons in the wrong order, and the next thing I know, I've changed the time instead of the year and date."

"You sound like my mother," Tina said. "Every time there's a power outage, I have to reset the clocks on the stove and the microwave."

Ashleigh turned her evil eye on them. She was obviously itching to say something, but she held her tongue. Maybe she didn't want to take Tina on again. I didn't blame her. Tina struck me as bossy, arrogant and, well, kind of bitchy.

"Give me your watch," Tina said to Carrie.

They both came to a halt, and Carrie handed over her watch. Tina fiddled with it for a few seconds before handing it back with a triumphant "All set." Carrie slipped the watch back onto her wrist.

By this time the line had advanced nearly thirty feet, and they ran to catch up without so much as a glance at the ground. Who knows what they might have missed.

Pretty soon my stomach started to grumble. I checked the time. Eleven thirty. We'd gathered at the muster site at seven. I wondered how much territory our quadrant held and how long it would take to finish searching it. Would we be allowed to stop for lunch? Would lunch be provided? Maybe the Sip 'n' Bite was bringing sandwiches for the volunteers. I loved their egg-salad sandwiches the best. Or maybe they'd ordered pizza.

I don't know what made me glance over at Charlie just then, but when I did, he wasn't there. I stopped and turned around to look for him. I spotted him a good thirty feet behind the rest of the line. He was standing perfectly still, head bowed. His hands hung limply at his sides, and he seemed to be staring at the ground in front of him.

While the rest of my line advanced, I walked back to see what was wrong with Charlie. I was careful to retrace my steps so as not to disturb anything else. I scanned the ground as I walked, looking for whatever had caught his attention, but I didn't see anything.

"You okay, Charlie?" I asked.

He swallowed hard without looking up. Then abruptly he spun around, ran back several paces and threw up. I picked my way to where he had been standing.

When I got a little closer, I saw a big dip in the terrain. A step or two closer still, and I saw a flash of color. Navy blue. Another step. The navy blue turned out to be a jacket. A glint of silver on one exposed wrist—a watch with a face so shattered I couldn't read the time. I saw jeans. Then boots. She lay faceup on the ground. She wasn't moving. She wasn't ever going to move again.

I took a deep breath before I allowed my eyes to travel up the body to the head. Right away I knew why Charlie had been sick. Shoulder-length chestnut hair matted with something dark and crusted covered most of her face, leaving only her chin and her neck visible, both impossibly white. That was probably a blessing, given the insects crawling in the blood.

I don't know how long I stood there staring at her. Probably not long. Probably not more than a few seconds. But it was long enough to burn the image of her into my brain and start me trembling all over.

I felt my breakfast rise in my throat, but I fought it
back down. I turned my back on her, breathed in and
out deeply a couple of times to steady myself and
called for a halt in a voice that I hoped conveyed
nothing more than another cigarette butt or foil
gum wrapper.

The line stopped.

The first time someone had spotted something—
the glint of a pop can, as it turned out—everyone
in the line had buzzed with excitement. But that
was a long time and too many finds ago. This time
no one buzzed. Everyone just stood silently in line
and waited for the next useless piece of trash to be
collected. They didn't even bother to watch what was
going on while word filtered to the officer in charge
of our quadrant.

Except for Carrie.

Her two friends were using the stop to carry on
a conversation, Tina with her hands on her hips, her
whole posture giving off an air of impatience, and
Desiree leaning in to listen, her shoulders rounded,
her pose submissive. Carrie slowly made her way
back to where I was. She showed the good sense to

retrace her own steps for most of the way, and she was frowning. I especially remember that.

She looked at me as she came to a stop, and then she slowly lowered her head to see what had stopped Charlie and me. All the color left her face, and one hand flew up to her mouth. She swallowed hard, fighting the urge to vomit, but she couldn't seem to take her eyes off what she was looking at. I had to take her by the elbow to stop her from getting too close.

Ashleigh was the next to break the line, much to the disapproval of a couple of women beside her who reminded her of what we had been told—whenever the line stops, stay put.

"My friend just barfed back there," Ashleigh said. She didn't seem the slightest bit intimidated. "Someone has to help him." At least she took a circuitous route to Charlie, then put an arm around him, looked at the ground where he had been sick, said, "Eeew!" and turned away immediately. It took her another minute or two before she got her gag reflex under control and was able to comfort Charlie, who looked as if he had been dipped in bleach.

Detective Martin finally broke through the stopped search line.

"What have we got this time?" It may have been my imagination, but he sounded less than enthusiastic about the prospects.

Carrie opened her mouth to answer.

"Don't," I hissed at her. "We don't want everyone stampeding over here to take a look. Let him handle it."

She closed her mouth again and kept it shut.

Detective Martin's face became pinched with annoyance when neither of us answered him. He fixed his gaze on me. "Riley?"

I shook my head.

He swore softly under his breath. I wasn't his favorite person at the best of times, and this was serious business. He stopped beside Carrie and me and looked down at the ground. His face froze into the mask I knew all too well, a cop at work. He took out his cell phone and spoke quietly into it, keeping his tone flat, never once mentioning Alicia or a body.

Aunt Ginny showed up a few minutes later, and she and Detective Martin squatted next to the body. Aunt Ginny made a second phone call.

Uniformed officers were deployed to shepherd the volunteers out of the woods, and another cop—a forensics officer—began to secure the scene so that he could take photographs and collect evidence.

Everyone was buzzing again as we made our way back to search headquarters. I walked arm in arm with Charlie, who was shakier and even paler after being sick than he had been before. He also smelled of vomit. Ashleigh, on the other side of me to avoid Charlie's odor, demanded to know what was going on. I whispered into her ear and warned her not to say a word. For once she managed to keep a piece of hot news to herself.

Carrie was in front of us, flanked by Tina and Desiree. Each was holding one of her elbows, and I could see that they were bearing some of her weight. Ashleigh shook her head in disgust.

"What a drama queen," she muttered. "It's just like her to try to suck up all the attention. Trust me, if she'd been the one to find Alicia instead of Charlie, she'd have made a scene you'd never forget. I bet she'd even end up on the news. Maybe she still will." Her venom surprised me.

As we emerged from the woods, I searched out the police van. A couple of cops were standing beside it, cups of coffee in their hands. An older man, a civilian I assumed was Mr. Allen, was sitting in the van with the door open, a can of soda propped up against the seat. He was turned sideways in the passenger seat so that he had a good view of the woods. When he saw us all marching toward him, he grabbed his cane and maneuvered himself onto the ground. I watched him hobble over to the two cops, both of whom were at full alert now, watching us approach like a wave. One of them was on his phone, presumably being told what we had just discovered. Mr. Allen went straight to that cop and said something, but as far as I could tell, the cop didn't answer. It was probably against protocol to say anything until a positive identification had been made. Not, in my opinion, that one was needed. The body out there had to be Alicia. Except for the backpack, which I hadn't seen, it matched her description.

It wasn't long before the other search parties trickled back to HQ, Mrs. Allen among them. She scanned the crowd for her husband and hurried to him. I heard her say, "What happened? Did they find something?"

All her husband could do was shake his head. So far no one had told him anything.

Aunt Ginny and the police chief were grim-faced when they appeared. They walked directly to Mr. and Mrs. Allen and led them far from the crowd. I can't say for sure, but I bet that everyone out there turned to look, trying to read faces and gestures to find out what had happened. Not that you needed to be an expert in interpreting body language to figure it out. Only a moment later, Mrs. Allen said, "No, no, no!" in an anguished voice. Mr. Allen, leaning heavily on his cane, put his free arm around her. His head was bowed. That's when everyone knew that Alicia had been found but that she hadn't been found alive.

THREE

Everyone was shocked by the way things had turned out. Even though Alicia had been missing for three days, I think most people had believed that even if she was hurt, she would be alive, and that whatever had happened to her, she would be all right. The terrible news rippled through the crowd, and everyone continued to watch the Allens, clinging to each other as they listened to the chief.

More cop cars arrived. So did the media. As for the volunteers, nobody wanted to leave without knowing exactly what was going on. We milled around search headquarters for a good thirty minutes before

Detective Martin finally called us together, thanked us all for our hard work and told us we would be escorted from the site by uniformed officers so as to minimize any further contamination of what was now a death-investigation scene. Ashleigh announced she was starving and wanted to go to the Sip 'n' Bite for something to eat. I still felt queasy from what I had seen, and Charlie's face was still chalky. He had no appetite. We walked him home, asked him a dozen times if he was okay, heard him say he was, even though he didn't look it, and left him on his porch. I went to the Sip 'n' Bite for a mug of ginger tea and turned away when Ashleigh doused her fries in blood-red ketchup.

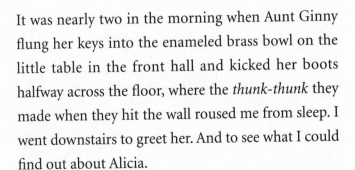

It was nearly two in the morning when Aunt Ginny flung her keys into the enameled brass bowl on the little table in the front hall and kicked her boots halfway across the floor, where the *thunk-thunk* they made when they hit the wall roused me from sleep. I went downstairs to greet her. And to see what I could find out about Alicia.

"She was murdered, right?" I asked. That's what it had looked like to me. Judging from the amount of blood matted into her hair and congealed around her head, and the absence of any indication of something having, say, fallen on her accidentally, it looked as if someone had bludgeoned her. Or shot her. The thought of either made me queasy all over again.

"It's a homicide, yes," Aunt Ginny said. "And I'm on the case."

"Lead?" I asked. Being lead detective on a homicide case was everything Aunt Ginny had ever wanted. She had been working toward that goal for her entire adult life.

"Well, no." She shrugged off her jacket and tossed it onto the couch in the living room before heading for the fridge and pulling out a tub of caramel ice cream. She grabbed a spoon from the utensil drawer and sat down at the kitchen table to dig in.

"Did you know this girl, Riley?"

"I knew *of* her." I told her everything I knew.

"Josh says you were the one to call him."

"Charlie was the one who found her."

"I know." She looked me over. "What I mean is, are you okay? Finding…something like that, it can be pretty traumatic."

"I'm okay, Aunt Ginny," I said. But if I had it to do over again, knowing what I now knew, I never would have left that line.

"Is Charlie okay?"

"He was pretty shaky when Ashleigh and I left him at home. I hope he's okay."

Aunt Ginny nodded and dug her spoon into the ice cream to extract a particularly rich vein of caramel. "Josh says there was another girl with you. Carrie Denison."

"That's right."

"What was she doing there?"

"I don't know. I guess she noticed Charlie and me and got curious. I think she regrets it. She was shaking harder than Charlie."

"Did anyone else come and look at the body before Josh showed up?"

"No."

Aunt Ginny nodded, and I knew she had committed to memory everything I'd told her about

Alicia and how we'd found her. Before she did anything else, she would take out her notebook and write it all down. She put the lid on the ice cream and put it back in the freezer.

"Go to bed," Aunt Ginny said. "It'll be time for school before you know it."

Moorebridge woke up Monday morning to the news that Alicia Allen had been bludgeoned on the head and left for dead. The weapon, something consistent with a tree branch, most likely a piece of windfall, had so far not been located. According to the pathologist, the blows had caused bleeding in her brain. It had taken Alicia several hours to die. The police chief assured the public that everything possible was being done to locate and bring Alicia's killer to justice. In the meantime, parents were warned to keep an eye on their children, and everyone, especially young females, was warned to exercise extreme caution and, as much as possible, avoid walking alone. Everyone was advised to stay clear of the woods until further notice.

School was chaotic. A lot of kids had volunteered to search for Alicia, and they all spun stories for the kids who hadn't volunteered. It didn't matter what they had actually seen or even if they had seen anything at all. They had been there, and therefore they had something to report. My homeroom teacher broached the topic of Alicia's death, and as part of the announcements that morning we were told (a) that grief counselors would be available, should anyone feel the need to talk to one, and (b) the police would be at school gathering information as part of their investigation into Alicia's murder. Anyone who knew Alicia and/or had any information relevant to her death should cooperate with police.

Sure enough, I caught glimpses of both Aunt Ginny and Detective Martin as I went through the day. Once they were out in the schoolyard talking to kids, mostly older kids. Another time I saw them in the school office, where they were talking to the principal.

"I don't know what the big mystery is," Ashleigh grumbled at lunch. "If you ask me, Carrie did it."

"Carrie Denison?" I stared at her. "What makes you think that?"

"Well, first of all, Carrie hated Alicia's guts. I know. I saw them in a catfight the day before Alicia disappeared. Carrie threatened to kill Alicia."

"*What*? No way. It was probably just a figure of speech."

"Uh-uh. This was the real deal," Ashleigh said. "I heard her. *And* saw her. She meant what she said. She shoved Alicia around. She was getting really physical."

"Over what?"

"Over the announcement about the youth orchestra."

"Huh?"

"Seriously?" Ashleigh shook her head, incredulous. "How do you not know this? Everyone was talking about it."

"You weren't," I said. "Not until now."

Ashleigh ignored the comment. "Alicia and Carrie both play violin."

"I know."

"They were both in the school orchestra, both in the regional orchestra, and they both tried out for the national youth orchestra."

That I didn't know. In fact, I didn't even know there was a national youth orchestra. Ashleigh had to enlighten me about that as well.

"You have to audition for it, and it's really competitive," she continued. "To be in it at their age is a big deal, because they're the youngest players. And you have to be better than good to get in, Riley. You're up against kids from the city whose parents send them to private lessons and conservatories, kids who are obsessive about practising. But if you get in, and if you're good and you work hard, you're practically guaranteed to get accepted into the music program of your choice when you graduate high school. And the national youth orchestra is supposedly one of the best anywhere. It tours. It's even done some recordings."

"And both Carrie and Alicia are—or were—good enough to try out for it?" I asked. Everyone knew Alicia was a natural. But Carrie? I'd seen Carrie goofing around at school with her buddies Tina and Desiree. She struck me as a total lightweight, more interested in shopping and gossiping than anything else. I had trouble picturing her being serious enough about anything, let alone the violin, to actually excel at it.

"Both of their mothers boast about them to my mother every time they come into the store." Ashleigh's parents were pharmacists and operated a drugstore on Moorebridge's main street.

"So they were fighting about playing violin?"

Ashleigh rolled her eyes. "They were fighting over a spot in the youth orchestra. They both auditioned for it. They both wanted it. Alicia got it. It was announced on Monday."

"And?"

Ashleigh shook her head in exasperation. "Really? Are you really not getting this?"

"Are you telling me that Alicia got picked, and Carrie was—what?—so insanely jealous that she killed her?"

"That's exactly what I'm telling you. Carrie claims that Alicia got the position because Mr. Todd pressured the head of the youth orchestra to give it to her. And because Mr. Todd is such a big deal—"

"Okay, wait a minute." I stopped her right there. "Mr. Todd is a big deal?" He was the music teacher at our school, a middle-aged, slightly hunched man with an intense stare. I wasn't in any of his classes.

I didn't take music. But I had heard about him and his high standards, which meant a lot of practicing for kids in the school orchestra.

Ashleigh rolled her eyes again. "Mr. Todd has a lot of pull. That's what everyone says."

"What?" I demanded. "No offense to anyone, I'm sure, but he teaches music at a regional high school pretty much in the middle of nowhere. If he was such a big deal, at a bare minimum he'd be teaching at some private school somewhere. More likely, he wouldn't be teaching school at all. He'd be teaching at some prestigious conservatory somewhere."

"Riley, Riley, Riley." She shook her head. "Mr. Todd came highly recommended. He's supposed to be one of the best music teachers in the country. A lot of his previous students are successful professional musicians now."

"Then what's he doing up here?"

"He got sick. I don't know all the details, but he had to give up conducting."

"He was a conductor?"

"Yes. But it was too much pressure for him. And then his sister died, and he was named guardian for her son. That's why he moved up here. To take care of Simon."

"Simon?"

"Simon Phillips."

"The piano player?"

The Simon Phillips who went to our school was eighteen and in his last year of school. I knew who he was because during the second or third week of the semester, I made what turned out to be the huge mistake of dropping a textbook in the hallway outside the music room. The book—biology—was one of those brick-like tomes that tugs you backward after you put it in your backpack. The book hit the ground with an explosive bang that echoed in the hallway, which up until that very minute had been filled with the sweet strains of piano music. I don't know the name of the piece, but it was classical, and it sounded beautiful.

The instant I dropped the book—accidentally, as I was forced to explain over and over again—the music stopped. I heard footsteps. The door to the music room flew open and a tall, skinny, red-faced boy appeared. He ripped into me for ruining his practice. Didn't I know better than to make noise in the hallway when someone was quite obviously practising? Was I trying to destroy his concentration? What was I doing up there, anyway? There were no lockers in the hall outside the music room. Who did I think I was? Et cetera, et cetera.

To say he was angry would be an understatement. He was enraged. He was still yelling at me after I had apologized, after I had explained for the fifth time that it was an accident, and after I had slunk down the hall to the stairs. I found out later from Charlie that his name was Simon and that, yes, he was weird and kind of anal. But that he was also a musical prodigy, which was supposed to explain his weirdness, although, in Charlie's opinion, Simon was just full of himself. All the praise had gone to his head and made him stuck up and holier than thou. It also explained why he looked down his long nose at everyone else, not only in school but also in town, and probably in the whole county—at least according to Charlie.

"Yes, the piano player," Ashleigh said in answer to my question. "And listen to this. I heard that Simon only became as good as he is after Uncle Richard—

Mr. Todd—took over his care. I don't know if it's true, but I heard he practices six or eight hours a day. I don't even know how that's possible unless he doesn't sleep."

All of which I had to admit was interesting, but… "What does Simon have to do with Alicia?" I asked.

Ashleigh sighed. "I wasn't talking about Simon. I was talking about his uncle. And I wasn't really talking about him either except to say that, according to Carrie, he got the first violin position for Alicia. Carrie accused her of being teacher's pet."

I shook my head. I like music as much as the next person. Maybe more. After all, I more or less grew up on my Grandpa Jimmy's tour bus. Jimmy was a rock star back in the sixties and had a loyal following up until the day he died suddenly of a heart attack. Jimmy and the guys put on a great show, and it wasn't unusual for old fans to drag their kids to see them and for those kids to become big fans too. Jimmy's love of music was infectious. But I doubt it would ever have crossed his mind to get even with a competitor by literally knocking him off.

"It doesn't seem like much of a motive for murder, Ashleigh."

She studied the doubt on my face. "You have to understand Carrie," she said. "She has a temper. A serious temper. When she gets mad, she throws things. I heard there are dents all over the walls of her bedroom from where she punched them. She slapped a girl once, so hard that the girl had a handprint on her cheek for two days. She's exactly the kind of person who would get so angry about losing out to Alicia that she'd turn violent." She reflected for a few seconds. "If you ask me, she definitely did it."

FOUR

I was on my way to school the next morning when someone called my name. I braked and looked around.

"Over here."

Carrie Denison waved at me from the alley between the hardware store and the real estate office next to it. I backed up and got off my bike.

She looked different than she usually did. Grayer somehow. Maybe it was the complete lack of makeup—no mascara, eye shadow, blusher or lipstick to brighten her face. Maybe it was the insipid yellow sweater she was wearing. It made her skin look sallow.

Her hair, which was usually thick and glossy, lay limp and flat around her head. She was pale and drawn, as if she'd been having trouble sleeping. Maybe she was reliving what she had seen in the woods on Sunday morning.

"I need to talk to you," she said. "But not here."

"Talk to me? About what?"

"The cops questioned me yesterday. They think I did it. They think I killed Alicia."

"Oh." I didn't know what else to say. I didn't even know why she was telling me this.

She glanced around nervously. "You know the little park next to the Legion?"

I nodded.

"Meet me there in five minutes."

"I have school."

"Please? I need your help."

I'm pretty sure my mouth was open as I stared at her. "I don't even know you."

"Five minutes. Please," she said. She disappeared down the alley before I could reply.

I debated whether to follow her. For sure it would mean being late for school, and that would mean a trip to Mr. Chen's office to offer an explanation and get a late slip. It took all of two seconds for curiosity to get the better of me. I jumped on my bike and was at the park before she was. We sat on a bench as far from the road as possible.

"I know you don't know me," Carrie said. "But I've heard about you. Everybody has. You solved Ethan Crawford's murder. And you figured out what happened to Mr. Goran. I need help to prove I didn't kill Alicia."

"If you really are a suspect, Carrie, then you're going to need a good lawyer," I said. "This is serious."

"I know it's serious." She looked evenly at me, and I saw a steeliness in her eyes that surprised me. She looked hard somehow, not like the usual ditz I sometimes glimpsed around school. "That's why I'm talking to you. I don't think the cops are the only ones who think I did it."

"What do you mean? What about your parents?"

"What about them?" Her tone was dismissive.

"They believe you."

"Do they?"

"I'm sure they do. They're your parents." They had to believe her. That's what parents did, right? They believed in their kids, and they stuck by them, no matter what.

She hesitated and looked down at her feet. It was a full minute before her eyes met mine again. Her whole body was stiff, and her knuckles white where she clasped her hands on her lap. "Not many people know this, but they're not really my parents."

"You're adopted?"

"Marion, my mom—well, I refer to her as my mom, but I always call her Marion. Some of my friends can't believe I call my parents by their first names, but she's not my mom. She was my real mom's best friend. My real mom and dad were both only children. And their parents were also only children. Weird, huh?"

"Families are a lot smaller than they used to be."

"Yeah, well mine was so small that when my parents were killed in a car accident when I was two, there were no relatives to take me. My grandparents were dead. There were no uncles or aunts. No cousins. Just good old Marion, who became my legal guardian. Marion always wanted kids, but she couldn't have any no matter what she tried. Then my parents died, and she got me. She called me her daughter right from the start."

"Right. Like I said. So you're adopted."

"Sort of, I guess. But not really. Marion and Edward never legally adopted me."

"How come?" Adoption seemed like the natural next step when a woman was already calling an orphan her daughter.

"I don't know. I think it has something to do with Edward, but I don't know what." She didn't sound happy. "Things were pretty good until I got to be about twelve. Then…I don't know. All of a sudden everything I did got on Marion's nerves. She's never come right out and said it, but I think she regrets taking me in."

"What about your dad…I mean, Edward?"

"He's okay. He's kind of sweet. But he's never gotten too involved with me. He leaves everything to Marion. I think he's a little afraid of me. Of me being a girl, you know? When the cops showed up at the house, he let her do all the talking. When he looked at me, which I think he did maybe once the whole time the cops were there, it was like the sight of me made his eyes hurt. And Marion—all she cares about is how horrible this whole thing is for her. She's mortified that the police seem to think I killed someone, and she's convinced that everyone thinks she's a terrible mother because otherwise how did she end up with a murderer living under her roof? She says she doesn't know how she'll be able to hold her head up when she goes into town. She'll probably pray that people will forgive her for raising something like me."

"It can't be that bad," I said.

She fixed me with a frank, somewhat superior look. "Really? Do you think I would be talking to you about this if I had parents who were one hundred percent in my corner?"

"What about your friends? They must believe in you."

"Tina and Desiree? Maybe. But what are they going to do about it? Nothing. It would never occur to them to do anything." Her eyes searched mine. "Will you help me?"

What did she think I could do that the police weren't already doing? Or was she scared of tunnel vision—of the cops building a case against her based on their suspicions instead of on the facts? Everyone knew that happened sometimes.

"You said the police questioned you."

She nodded.

"I want you to tell me everything they said to you and everything you said to them."

Another curt nod.

"Who questioned you?"

"Taylor's dad." Taylor Martin goes to our school. Her dad is Josh Martin.

"Was he alone, or did he have another detective with him?"

"Your aunt was there too." She said it matter-of-factly, as if she didn't hold it against me that my aunt was trying to put her in prison. "But Taylor's dad did most of the talking. He was kind of annoying, you know, the way he wouldn't let your aunt say anything."

No surprise there.

"What did he say?"

"At first he was kind of like a priest or something. He kept telling me that I would feel much better if I got everything off my chest and told him the truth. But I was telling the truth. I had nothing to do with what happened to Alicia."

"He didn't believe you?"

"He kept trying to get me to say that I was jealous of Alicia. And he said that he understood how I felt because he'd heard about the competition and he knows how important it was to both of us to win, and what a blow it must have been to come in second. He did all that psychology stuff, you know, trying to convince me that he was on my side. He said I probably didn't mean to kill Alicia. I probably lost my temper and just lashed out at her, and he understood that. He said it would be best for everyone, especially Alicia's parents, if I told the truth. He said it would help them find closure."

"*Were* you jealous of her?"

"Of course I was. Anyone who says they weren't jealous of her is lying. Everything came easy to Alicia. Everything. But I was angrier with Mr. Todd. Alicia was his pet. She only got the spot because he promoted her to the selection committee. I told her if she was as fair as she always pretended to be, she would ask for a reaudition for both of us without Mr. Todd."

"And?"

"She said, and I quote, *I don't think that will be necessary*. And, yeah, I lost my temper. I shoved her.

I wanted to do worse. I knew it was wrong when I was doing it, but I couldn't stop myself, even though I knew someone was watching us. That friend of yours. Ashleigh Wainwright. I guess she ratted me out to the police." She looked me square in the eye. "But I didn't kill Alicia."

"Do you have an alibi for when she was killed?"

She shook her head. "If I'd known I was going to be accused of murder, I would have made sure I was out in public making a spectacle of myself so that dozens of people would have remembered seeing me. I was at home. My parents weren't. They didn't get back until late. I didn't talk to anyone, and no one saw me. I just did my homework and practiced. As usual."

One more strike against her.

"Did Taylor's dad mention physical evidence or anything else?"

She gave me a blank look.

"Fingerprints on the murder weapon, the victim's blood on your clothes, a footwear impression in the woods—stuff like that. Did he mention any physical evidence that puts you at the scene of the crime?"

She shook her head, but I knew that cops like to play their cards close to the chest, and they always hold something back. Always. So just because they didn't mention something, that didn't mean they didn't know about it.

"But he did keep asking me about time," she said. "What time did I leave school? What time did I get home? How do I know for sure that it was before five o'clock? How do I know it wasn't later? Could it have been a few minutes later? Well, sure, I guess. I mean, I knew I got home around four thirty, because I'd been home for a few minutes before I decided to microwave a snack. That's when I saw the time. Well, then he wanted to know exactly how long I'd been home. Was it five minutes? Ten? Could it have been fifteen?"

"So he was really focused on five o'clock?" I wondered what he was basing that on. Alicia's watch, which had been broken? An eyewitness? Some other information that the police were keeping quiet about for now?

"Was he ever." She shuddered. "He can be really scary too. I mean, at first he was kind of nice, telling me he understood how it must feel to be constantly outdone by someone, how hard it is to be passed over. But later on he started to get kind of mad at me."

"What about witnesses? Did he mention or even hint that they have someone who might have seen you following Alicia or seen you go into the woods the day she disappeared?"

Anger sparked in her eyes. "Well, that would be impossible," she said. "Because I didn't follow her. I didn't even set foot in the woods. So anyone who says they saw me anywhere near there—and as far as I know no one has said anything like that—is lying."

"Okay." I thought for a moment. "Do you know anyone else who had a grudge against Alicia or was mad at her for some reason?"

"Little Miss Perfect? You've got to be kidding. Everyone treats her as if she's an angel come down to earth."

"An angel who someone bludgeoned to death," I pointed out.

Carrie looked down. "I know it doesn't sound good, but will you help me?"

I told her that I would think about it.

I got to school late—no surprise there—suffered Mr. Chen's sarcasm, picked up a late slip and was on my way to my locker when the class-change bell rang. Amid the sudden flood of students in the halls, I glimpsed Aunt Ginny. She and Josh Martin were marching up to the third floor with Mr. Chen. Two uniformed officers followed them. What was going on?

I wasn't the only person asking that question. The four cops drew a lot of attention. One by one at first, and then bunch by bunch, students trailed them, until a sizable crowd filled the hall outside the cops' final destination—the music room. Aunt Ginny, Josh Martin and Mr. Chen entered the room. The uniformed officers were stationed outside the door to make sure no one interfered.

"There's nothing to see here, people," one of the uniforms said. "Go back to your classes."

No one moved. We had a fifteen-minute break before the bell rang again.

The uniform, whose name was Sharpe, had to be close to retirement age. Aunt Ginny had once pointed him out to me as the worst kind of cop—the kind with no ambition. He stood with his hands on his hips and an exasperated expression on his face. "Come on, people. You heard me. Back to class."

I had wormed my way to the front of the crowd, directly under Officer Sharpe's nose. I glanced over my shoulder. Nobody dispersed.

Officer Sharpe reached for his radio handset, but he didn't get a chance to use it because just then Detective Martin and Aunt Ginny emerged from the music room with Mr. Chen. Aunt Ginny was holding something in her hand—a sheet of notebook paper that had been slipped into a plastic evidence bag.

"Excuse me, excuse me, excuse me." The voice, sharp-edged with frustration, grew louder and louder until finally Mr. Todd, the music teacher, successfully elbowed his way to the top of the stairs and to the front of the crowd.

"Ah," said Mr. Chen. "Here's Mr. Todd now. He should be able to answer your questions."

I stepped aside to let the music teacher pass. Well, actually, he pushed me out of his way. That's when

Aunt Ginny spotted me. She shot me the evil eye. I pretended not to notice.

"What is going on?" Mr. Todd demanded. "Mrs. Dekes informed me that you were searching my classroom. Really, Mr. Chen, you should have called me first."

"Would you please step into the music room, sir?" Aunt Ginny asked.

Mr. Todd glared at her. "And you are?"

"Detective McFee."

"Well, Detective McFee, I am not at all happy with your performance. Surely you're obliged to notify the appropriate parties before you conduct a search."

"I did." Aunt Ginny's tone was curt and peeved. "Mrs. Dekes is responsible for this school and its facilities."

"But she is not, I assure you, responsible for my music room and its instruments, which had better not have been damaged…"

Aunt Ginny shook her head wearily. Doubtless she had dealt with people like Mr. Todd before, and clearly it was not her favorite part of the job. But she said nothing and looked to Mr. Chen for help.

Mr. Chen touched Mr. Todd's arm. "Richard, we need you inside the music room."

Mr. Todd opened his mouth, probably to protest, but then seemed to think better of it. He glanced at the students massed behind him and, without another word, followed Mr. Chen into the music room. Detective Martin and Aunt Ginny went with them. They were still inside, behind closed doors, when the bell rang and we all had to leave. We had no choice, not after Mrs. Dekes appeared at the bottom of the stairs and issued a warning that anyone late for the next class would get a detention.

Who knows how news gets around as fast as it does in a school? Who knows how much of it is true? By lunch, everyone was talking about what the police had supposedly found in the music room and what it meant. When Ashleigh arrived at my locker, she was bursting to share what she had overheard in the second-floor girls' washroom.

"Carrie's nowhere near as smart as you think she is." She was gloating, as if she was about to prove conclusively something she'd been saying all along. "You know why the cops were called? Because someone found a note."

Charlie showed up just then.

"What note? What are you talking about?" he asked. He was clutching an oversized brown paper bag. Charlie brought his lunch every day—delicious homemade sandwiches on homemade bread (Charlie's mother loved her bread maker), veggies, a piece of fruit and some other homemade treat. Charlie's lunches were always, always mouthwatering. His mother was an excellent cook who had taken more first prizes in the preserves and baking categories at the annual agricultural fair than anyone else in town.

"The cops were here," Ashleigh said. "You didn't know?"

I grabbed my lunch and closed my locker. We started for the stairs.

"Let's eat outside," I said. It was a sunny, unseasonably warm day.

"What about the cops?" Charlie asked. "What did they want? Was it about Alicia?"

"It sure was," Ashleigh said.

I pushed open the door at the bottom of the stairs, and we stepped out into the sun at the rear of the school.

Ashleigh eyed Charlie's lunch bag. "What kind of sandwich did your mom make today?"

"Roast beef."

"Mustard or mayo?"

"Honey mustard."

Ashleigh licked her lips. Whenever Charlie's sandwich sounded or looked especially delicious, she shamelessly begged for half or a quarter or, if Charlie held firm, which he usually did, just a single bite.

"Give me half of your sandwich and I'll tell you the whole story."

Charlie shook his head. "Riley will tell me for free."

"Sorry, Charlie. I don't know the whole story. Ashleigh was just about to tell me."

Ashleigh smiled triumphantly and stuck out her hand for her bribe. Charlie tightened his grip on his lunch bag.

"I don't think I care that much," he said.

Ashleigh crossed her arms over her chest. "In that case, no one hears the whole story."

"Fine with me."

"Fine with me too," I said. "I might be able to worm something out of Aunt Ginny, especially if I bribe her with homemade pie." I had started making pies during the summer, when there was plenty of fresh fruit available. Aunt Ginny went positively weak at the knees when I pulled one out of the oven and served it à la mode.

Ashleigh's gloat turned into a pout.

"You guys are no fun!" She glowered at us, especially Charlie. "Okay, fine. Lydia Teasdale—do you know her?" Charlie nodded. I had no idea who she was. "She's in junior band," Ashleigh said. "She plays trumpet. Anyway, Mr. Todd handed out music for a piece they're supposed to learn. Lydia and a guy, I think it was Anthony Fairburn, were in there on a spare, practicing, and Lydia found a note inside her music. It was about Alicia, saying she was a stuck-up bitch and—get this—that the person who wrote the note wanted to kill her. And the kicker? It was written the day *after* the announcement about the youth orchestra and the day *before* Alicia was killed."

"How do they know that?" I asked.

"Because the idiot who wrote it put the date at the top. I heard there was a dagger drawn around it, with blood dripping off it."

"Next you're going to tell me that the note was signed," I said.

"It was!" When Charlie and I both stared at her, stunned, she said, "Well, sort of. There was a big *C* at the bottom of the note." She paused to gauge our reaction. "Don't you get it?" she said. "It was Carrie. Carrie wrote the note. Carrie admitted she wanted to kill Alicia."

"She probably didn't mean it," I said.

"Funny, though, that Alicia got killed the next day, don't you think?" Ashleigh said.

"Maybe someone else wrote the note and signed it with a *C*," Charlie said.

Ashleigh gave him a sour look. "For what possible reason?"

"I don't know. To get Carrie in trouble?"

"They took the note to the office," Ashleigh said. "They compared it to Carrie's signature in the files. And the *C* in the files looked just like the *C* on that note. They're going to send it to a handwriting expert for confirmation."

"How do you know all this?" I hadn't yet gotten over how much information Ashleigh was able to tap into, and how quickly.

"How do you not?" she asked. "It's all over the place. Everyone's on it." She gazed longingly at Charlie's lunch bag. "I'm starving," she groaned. "I have to get something to eat. I'll be right back." She went inside, and I heard her feet on the concrete stairs leading down into the cafeteria.

"It doesn't sound right to me," Charlie said. "If you're actually going to kill someone, why would you advertise that in advance by leaving a dated, signed note lying around?"

It was a good question.

FIVE

When Ashleigh returned with a tuna-salad sandwich and some carrot sticks from the cafeteria, we decided to do what a lot of other kids were doing—eat on the bleachers at the side of the school athletic field. It was fairly quiet outside, despite the whoops of a bunch of guys tossing a football around at the far end of the athletic field and the rhythmic *thunk-thunk-thunk* of a hammer being wielded by one of the school maintenance staff, who was down on his hands and knees near the farthest edge of the schoolyard. Each strike of the hammer made a dull echoey sound, as if he was hitting wood against wood. All around us were small groups of lunchers, each group just far enough from the others to foil eavesdropping—assuming no one shouted like Ashleigh did when I had finished telling her and Charlie about my encounter that morning with Carrie.

"So you're telling me that the reason you were late for school today was because Carrie Denison asked you to help her prove to the cops that she didn't kill Alicia Allen, despite overwhelming evidence proving it was her?"

"Except for the last part, yes."

Ashleigh shook her head in disgust. Charlie stopped munching his sandwich and stared wide-eyed at me.

"Do you believe her, Riley?" he asked.

"I don't know." That was the truth. "But she's scared, and I think she feels that everyone is against her. She says her parents are acting like they think she did it." I had no intention of betraying Carrie's confidence about Marion and Edward not really being her parents.

"That should tell you something," Ashleigh said. She turned to Charlie for confirmation. "She probably freaks out on them the way she freaked out on Alicia.

If her parents don't already know she did it, they must suspect. Otherwise they'd be mortgaging the house to hire the best criminal lawyer they could find."

"What are you talking about?" Charlie asked. "What do you mean, Carrie freaked out on Alicia?"

Ashleigh filled him in.

That reminded me. "She says she saw you, Ashleigh."

"How come you never mentioned it the whole time we were looking for Alicia?" Charlie sounded hurt by her omission.

"Because I didn't think anything had happened to her. And I had no idea that you were in love with Alicia."

Charlie's cheeks reddened. "I wasn't in love—"

"Or whatever." Ashleigh waved a hand to dismiss the topic.

I hesitated before I asked, "Did you tell the police what you saw?"

Ashleigh sighed. "I thought about it. But it felt so much like tattling. Do you think I should?"

"You have to," Charlie said.

"Somebody else already told them," I said. "Carrie says the cops asked her about it. Was anyone else there, Ashleigh?"

"Just Tina. But she wouldn't rat out her best friend." She paused. "Would she?" She let out another long sigh. "There was no one else around, Riley. And I swear I didn't tell the cops. If Tina did, it's probably because she thinks the same thing I do—Carrie did it. No one else had a motive. No one else actually hated the perfect Alicia Allen." She looked me over as she peeled the plastic wrap from her sandwich. "You're going to help her, aren't you?"

"She wouldn't have asked me if she wasn't desperate." That, of course, was no guarantee that she hadn't done it. But she'd seemed sincere to me. Sincere and scared and alone. "I just couldn't say no."

Ashleigh sighed. "I guess I'm not surprised. But seriously, Riley, who else besides Carrie would have wanted to kill Alicia? Everyone knows she was insanely jealous when Alicia got the last spot in the youth orchestra."

That was, of course, the jackpot question. I gazed out over the athletic field, which was when I saw them. I shoved my half-eaten sandwich back into my lunch bag and ran down the bleacher steps. "Meet at my locker after school," I called back to Ashleigh.

If she answered, I didn't hear her.

I caught up with Tina and Desiree just as they stepped off the athletic field and onto the ancient asphalt tarmac that surrounded the rear half of the school. I had to call Tina's name three times before I got her attention.

"What?" She spun around to see who was harassing her.

"I need to talk to you."

"Well, I don't need to talk to you." She turned away, grabbing Desiree by the elbow and dragging her along.

"Carrie asked me to help her," I called after them.

Desiree stopped to face me. "You talked to Carrie? I keep trying her cell, but I don't think it's turned on. When I called her house, no one answered. I left a message, but she never called me back. Is she all right?"

Tina shot her a scornful look. "She didn't talk to Carrie. She doesn't even know Carrie. Don't you know who she is? Her aunt is that new lady cop."

She turned vicious eyes on me. "Did your aunt send you to pump us for information? Because if she did, you're wasting your time. We're not going to help you send Carrie to prison."

"I spoke to her this morning." I focused on Desiree, who seemed more open to listening to me. "She asked me to help her. She says she didn't do it." I glanced at Tina. "You told the police about the shoving match between Carrie and Alicia, didn't you?"

Tina's face turned scarlet.

"What shoving match?" Desiree asked. "What are you talking about?" She turned to Tina. "What did you do, Tina? What did you tell the cops?"

"Nothing. I didn't tell them anything." Her eyes zeroed in on me. "If anyone ratted Carrie out, it was your friend Ashleigh."

"Ratted Carrie out?" Desiree's eyes brimmed with concern. "You're talking like you think she did it."

"Of course I don't think that." Tina glowered at me.

"What do you know about the note?" I asked.

"What note?" Tina said. "A fictional note she might have written to me?"

"You know what note. Everyone's been talking about it. The note that was found in the music room."

"I just know what I heard," Tina said.

"Did Carrie ever write you a note that said she wanted to kill Alicia?"

"So what if she did? Notes are notes."

"Did you tell the police about any of those notes?"

"I never saw a note like the one you're talking about."

"Who else did she pass notes to?"

"You're assuming she even passed that note," Tina said. "Maybe she wrote it and decided not to pass it. Maybe she was just fooling around."

"Do you and Carrie write a lot of notes?"

"They do in music class," Desiree said. Tina shot her a nasty look, which Desiree ignored. "Mr. Todd makes everyone shut off their cell phones and put them at the front of the room. A lot of people write notes in his class."

"Yeah." Tina crossed her arms over her chest as if that ended the matter. "A lot of people write notes in that class."

This was getting me nowhere. I tried another tack.

"Did either of you see Alicia after school the day she disappeared?"

"No." They said it in unison.

"What about Carrie?"

"I saw her at her locker after school," Tina volunteered, albeit grudgingly and only after Desiree turned to her to hear her answer.

"Did she say anything about where she was going or what she was going to do?"

"No. But she was in a hurry."

"You told me you saw her, but you didn't tell me that," Desiree said, frowning.

"Well, she was. I don't tell you every little thing, do I? Besides, I just remembered it now." She thought for a few seconds. "I saw Carrie at her locker after school. She was jamming stuff into her backpack. I waited for her, but she said she was in a rush and she was taking the back stairs."

The back stairs led to the athletic field. The road on the other side of the athletic field led, eventually, to the woods where Alicia had been found.

"That's all I know," Tina said. "I told the cops that same thing I just told you."

"She didn't say where she was going or what the rush was?"

Tina shook her head.

We were all silent. I glanced at Desiree, whose mouth hung open. She looked as if someone had just smacked her on the head.

"What about you?" I asked.

"Did I see Carrie or talk to her?" She shook her head. "I do Reading Buddies on Wednesdays, same as Alicia. I left school as soon as the bell rang so I could get to the library on time."

I'd heard of Reading Buddies. The whole school knew about it. It was a program run by the library. It recruited high school students to help kids in elementary school with their reading. Each volunteer met with their little charges twice a week. A lot of kids volunteered so they could get the community-service hours they needed to graduate.

"So Alicia was at the library that day?"

"She was supposed to be."

"Did you see her?"

Desiree shook her head. "But that doesn't mean anything. She could have been in a different room from me."

They had nothing else to tell me. Desiree asked me to say hi if I saw Carrie again. Tina just grunted.

I wondered where Carrie had been going in such a rush. She'd told me she'd gone home to do her homework. Had she lied to me?

Ashleigh was leaning against my locker, checking her phone, at the end of the school day. She pocketed the phone and moved aside when she saw me.

"Well?"

"Tina says she didn't tell the police about the shoving match. But they knew, Ashleigh."

"I swear I didn't tell them. Honest." She raised one hand as if she were taking an oath. "Although I'm not going to lie to you. I thought about it. Remember Monday when your aunt and Taylor's dad were at school all day, talking to all of Alicia's friends? I must have walked by the office ten times. I mean, you're supposed to tell them what you know, right? But I didn't, and I don't even like Carrie, so go figure."

"Tina says she didn't tell them either. But someone sure did. Was there anyone else around, Ashleigh? Did you see anyone watching besides Tina?"

Ashleigh shook her head. "And I'm pretty sure I would have noticed. The school was practically empty when it happened."

I wondered what my chances were of getting Aunt Ginny to tell me who that witness was.

"If you were going to kill someone, wouldn't you at least make sure you had an alibi?" I asked. "Carrie doesn't have one. She said so to the police."

"Maybe she doesn't have an alibi because she didn't know she was going to do it. Maybe it was a crime of passion. She found out that Alicia got the position, and she got angry and killed her without thinking."

"It's possible." When you came right down to it, almost anything was possible. "But seriously. Killing someone because they got a spot in a youth orchestra and you didn't?"

"Carrie wants to get into a good music program at university. She wants to be a professional musician. She already has the diva personality for it. Getting that spot in the orchestra would have given her a big advantage in getting accepted to the program of her choice. I hate to admit it, but the word is that she's pretty good."

"But Alicia was better."

"According to Mr. Todd she was. I guess he would know."

I made a mental note to talk to him too. He knew both girls from school and from the orchestra. He might have observed something between them that might help Carrie. Or that might hurt her. I knew Ashleigh thought I was crazy to believe Carrie, but I couldn't understand why she would ask me to help her prove her innocence if she had really done it.

I finished gathering my things and closed my locker.

"So, where are we going?" she asked.

"To the library. Alicia was supposed to volunteer the afternoon she disappeared. I want to find out if she showed up."

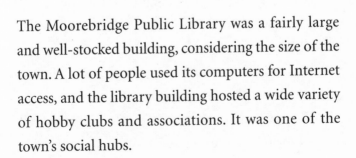

The Moorebridge Public Library was a fairly large and well-stocked building, considering the size of the town. A lot of people used its computers for Internet access, and the library building hosted a wide variety of hobby clubs and associations. It was one of the town's social hubs.

I went straight to the information desk to ask about the Reading Buddies program and was directed to Mrs. Burns in the children's department on the lower floor.

"Hey." Ashleigh came to an abrupt halt on the step in front of me. I almost fell over her. "That's Brendan Mitchell," she whispered. "Isn't he gorgeous? I babysit his little brother during the curling season." She waved and called out "Hi, Brendan. Hi, Zak" as she breezed over to them.

Brendan Mitchell was, as advertised, gorgeous—thick brown hair, wide shoulders, tall, lean and fit in blue jeans, a T-shirt and a leather jacket. He was squatting in front of a small boy, whom I took to be his little brother. The boy was crying. Brendan held him by both shoulders and spoke softly to him. Ashleigh crouched down beside Brendan.

"Hi, Zak." Her voice was soft and soothing.

Zak kept his chin where it was, on his chest. He gazed stubbornly at the floor.

"Hey, what's the matter?" Ashleigh asked him.

No answer. At least, not from Zak.

"Zak is sad," Brendan said. He squeezed his little brother's shoulder again. "I'm sad too, Zak.

So is Ashleigh. Everyone who knew Alicia is sad. But you know she would have wanted you to keep reading. You know how important that was to her."

Zak shook his head. "I don't want to read without Alicia."

"Mrs. Burns has someone else who is going to help you. Her name is Shawna. I know her. She's in my chemistry class. She's nice. You'll like her."

The little boy shook his head again. He crossed his arms firmly over his chest and looked down at the scuffed toes of his Velcro-sealed sneakers.

"Please, Zak?" Brendan said. "Just give it a try?"

The boy was a compact block of grumpy determination. He refused to budge.

"What if Ashleigh comes with us?" Brendan said, glancing at Ashleigh to see if she would agree.

Zak looked up tearfully at Ashleigh. She took one of his hands in hers. Brendan took the other and opened the door to the children's library. They were almost bowled over by a woman who rushed out without watching where she was going. Maybe she couldn't see properly. She was wearing dark glasses and a big floppy hat with a brim that fell over her forehead. Her head was bowed. She muttered, "Sorry" as she hurried past us.

Ashleigh clucked in disgust. "Well, excuse me, I'm sure," she muttered.

I stepped aside to give the woman clear access to the stairs and then followed Ashleigh and Brendan into the children's library.

Brendan went first to a woman at the service counter, Ashleigh a step behind, still holding Zak's hand. The woman at the counter, who I assumed was Mrs. Burns, bent down to speak to Zak. She pointed out a girl sitting at one of the library tables. I recognized the girl from school, but she was ahead of me, so I didn't know her. I'm not sure how Mrs. Burns did it, but she managed to convince Zak to meet Shawna. Brendan and Ashleigh walked him over, and Shawna either knew what she was doing or was just lucky, because after a couple of minutes Zak sat down at the table with her and the two of them started to talk. Brendan and Ashleigh came back to the desk.

"I think you can leave him," Mrs. Burns said. "It looks like he might be willing to give Shawna a chance."

"I think I'll wait outside," Brendan said. "Just in case."

Ashleigh looked longingly at Brendan as he left his brother and walked to the door, but she stayed with me. I introduced myself to Mrs. Burns.

"Are you interested in being a Reading Buddy?" she asked.

"Not exactly. I wanted to ask you about Alicia Allen."

Mrs. Burns sighed. "Dear Alicia. The children adored her." She nodded at a crayon drawing on her desk. "See this? One of the mothers dropped it off just a minute ago." I wondered if it was the woman in the floppy hat. "Her little boy did it. It's for Alicia, and as far as I know, that child was with her just the one time. That's the kind of impression she made on her little readers." She gazed at the picture and sighed. "I think I'll give it to Alicia's parents. And Alicia was doing a marvelous job with Zak too." She directed this to Ashleigh. "She really drew him out of his shell. I hope I can convince him not to give up."

"Was Alicia here last Wednesday, Mrs. Burns?"

The children's librarian shook her head. "The police asked me the same question. I wish she had been here. Then maybe what happened to her wouldn't have happened at all." She wiped a tear from the corner of one eye.

"Did she say why she couldn't make it?"

"That's the odd thing. Alicia was one of the most conscientious volunteers I've ever had. She almost never missed a session. She understood how important it was to show up regularly if she expected her reading buddies to take the program seriously. The one and only time she ever missed was when she was sick. She called that time to let me know. She called all of the kids' moms too to let them know."

"Did she call last week?"

She shook her head again. "But she sent a replacement." She nodded to Shawna, who was still talking to Zak. "It turns out she's a permanent replacement."

"You got her to agree to fill in for Alicia for the year?" I said.

"I didn't get her to agree. Alicia did. Apparently, Alicia recruited Shawna to take over for her. It's almost as if she knew something bad was going to happen to her." She shuddered.

"Did Alicia tell you why she decided to leave the program?"

"No. She never said a thing. It came as a complete surprise when Shawna showed up and told me she was subbing for Alicia. I kept expecting Alicia to call me and let me know what was going on. It didn't seem like her not to explain why she was quitting—and so suddenly." A few more tears appeared, and she blotted them with a tissue. "I'm going to miss her. She was great with the kids. She knew how to draw out the shy ones and keep the wilder ones under control. Her Saturday-morning story time was really popular. The children are really going to miss her."

Another little boy had joined Shawna and Zak, and the two boys were coloring a picture from one of the books on the table. Shawna stepped away from them long enough to tell me that she'd agreed to take over for Alicia. "I still need my community-service hours for graduation," she said. "Alicia told me all about Reading Buddies and said if I had a kid brother, which I do, then I'd be fine. She made it sound like fun. And, like I said, I need the hours to graduate."

"When exactly did Alicia ask you to take over for her?"

"Last week sometime."

"Do you remember which day?"

She thought for a moment. "Tuesday, I think."

"Are you sure it was Tuesday?" The day before she'd disappeared.

"Pretty sure. I was on my way to the dentist when she stopped me. I hate going to the dentist. You ever see that movie where the bad guy is a dentist who's really an ex-Nazi, and he tortures this guy by drilling holes in his teeth?" She shuddered at the thought.

"Did she say why she was quitting?" I asked.

Shawna shook her head. She obviously didn't know anything else.

So what did I know now that I didn't know before? The day before she'd been murdered, Alicia had decided to quit volunteering for Reading Buddies permanently. But why? And why hadn't she explained either to Mrs. Burns or to the girl she'd recruited to replace her?

I rejoined Ashleigh, and we left the children's library. Or, rather, I was following Ashleigh out the door of the children's library when she stopped dead in front of me—again.

"What now?" I asked.

"Look."

Brendan Mitchell was out in the hall waiting for Zak, just like he'd said he would. But he wasn't alone. Tina was with him. They were talking. Or, rather, Tina was talking and Brendan was looking at the library door, probably worrying about how his brother was doing.

I nudged Ashleigh. She started moving again, and when we reached Brendan she stopped and said, "It looks like Zak is settling in fine."

"I'm glad we ran into you, Ashleigh," Brendan said. "I wasn't making much progress until you showed up."

Ashleigh shot a triumphant look at Tina. "I was glad to help," she said.

Tina glowered at her.

Brendan flashed a smile of gratitude that seemed to buckle Ashleigh's knees. No doubt about it, he was a hot-looking guy. I bet a lot of girls were interested in him.

The children's library door opened. Mrs. Burns searched out Brendan.

"I don't know what happened," she said. "Everything seemed to be going smoothly when all of a sudden Zak started crying. He says he wants his brother. He says he wants to go home."

Brendan dashed into the library. Tina scowled.

"Thanks for nothing!" she said to Ashleigh. She started to go after Brendan, but he came out again before she reached the door. He was carrying Zak, who had wrapped his arms and legs around him. He was still crying.

"I want Alicia," he said over and over again.

"Hey, buddy," Brendan said softly. "We talked about that, remember?"

"I miss her."

"So do I," Brendan said. "So do I."

He walked past Tina without so much as glancing at her. He was too busy comforting Zak. Ashleigh snickered. Tina glared at her before hurrying after Brendan.

"Looks like Tina has a thing for Brendan," I said.

"Who doesn't?"

It made me wonder.

"Okay, so Alicia quit the Reading Buddies program and arranged for a replacement on Tuesday, the day before she disappeared. According to everyone who would know, she didn't come here after school the next day, and she didn't go home. So where did she go?"

"She must have gone to the woods," Ashleigh said.

"But why?"

Ashleigh had no answer.

We parted company. Ashleigh went home. I went over to Carrie's.

SIX

Carrie answered the door before I knocked and showed me through to the back porch. "None of the nosy neighbors can see us here," she said. "Did you find out anything?"

"The cops were at school today. They found a note you wrote. Haven't they talked to you about it yet?"

"What note?"

"I didn't see it, but the rumor is that someone found a note threatening to kill Alicia. It was written the day before Alicia died, and it was signed with a big *C*."

The color drained from her face.

"Did you write it, Carrie?"

"Where did they find it?"

"In the music room."

She slumped lower in her chair. "Oh my god."

"Apparently they sent it to a handwriting expert to see if it matches your handwriting."

"I'm dead." Carrie's voice was dull, flat, hopeless. "They're going to arrest me for sure."

"So it's true? You really wrote it?"

Her eyes met mine. "I wrote it, but I didn't mean it literally. I was just mad. It was right after Mr. Todd announced that Alicia got the first violin position, not me. But I didn't mean I was really going to kill her. People say stuff like that all the time. It never means anything."

"Unless the person ends up dead," I said. "Then people think it means a lot."

She moaned.

"Did you pass the note to anyone?"

"Tina."

"I asked Tina about the note. She says she never saw it."

Carrie's smile was barely perceptible. "She was just trying to protect me. But yeah, I wrote the note, and I passed it to Tina. She didn't like Alicia either."

"But she read it."

Carrie nodded.

"What did she do with it after that?"

"I don't know. I thought she'd thrown it out."

"Thrown it out where?"

"I don't know."

"The note was found inside some sheet music. How do you think it ended up there?"

"I don't know. You'll have to ask Tina what she did with it." She shook her head. "Do you think they really believe I meant what I wrote?"

"They might. Why did you put the date on it, and the dagger?"

"It was how I was feeling." She shrugged. "You have to tell them to talk to Tina. She'll tell them it's no big deal. We were always trashing Alicia. People are always trashing other people. You know what it's like at school."

I did. But this was different. This time someone had been murdered.

"I tried to get my parents to give me back my cell phone or at least let Tina or Desiree call the house. But they won't. Because it's something I want, they won't do it."

"I'll talk to Tina. But you have to level with me, Carrie. Is there anything else the police are going to find that you haven't told me about?"

"No, I swear. Riley, you have to believe me. I didn't kill Alicia. I was home all night. I wish I had someone to back me up, but I don't. I didn't know I was going to have to prove where I was. Nobody expects that."

I said it was okay. Then I asked her to tell me everything she could about the note.

"What do you mean?"

"Just what I said. Everything."

She drew in a deep breath. "We were in music class. The announcement about the youth orchestra had been made the night before, and Mr. Todd launched into this speech about how proud he was of Alicia for winning the spot, even though everyone knows how hard he promoted her and how much he favored her. He went on and on about how Alicia was a natural talent, but that she didn't try to coast on that, she practiced all the time, she put her music first, she realized that was the only way to get ahead. He looked at me when he said it, like he thought I don't practice enough. But I do. I put in a couple of hours every night."

That surprised me. Sure, I knew she was in the regional youth orchestra. I knew she'd had to try out to get in, so that meant she had to be pretty good. But the way she cruised around school with her buddies, sniping at girls she didn't think were cool enough— well, that just didn't compute with someone who cared more about her music than anything else.

"It made me angry. So I wrote that note to Tina. If I'd known the police were going to use it against me in a murder case, I never would have written it. But I didn't know because I had no intention of killing anyone. I was just venting. I was angry, that's all."

"But you said it was Mr. Todd who influenced whoever made the decision. Why weren't you angry at him instead?"

"Because Alicia did everything she could to suck up to him. She took lessons from him. She wormed her way into his family."

"His family?"

"Simon. You probably don't know him."

"I know who he is."

"He's all about his music. His life ambition is to be a concert pianist, and the word is that he has the talent and the contacts to make it. Alicia knew it. That's why she hung out with him so much. She's the only person in school who can stomach him—at least, that's what she wanted everyone to think. If you ask me, she only got close to him to get Mr. Todd's attention. Simon used to invite her over for dinner all the time. They were best buddies. What chance does that give someone like me? Simon looked down at everyone else in school, especially anyone in the school orchestra. He was slightly nicer to me when I made it into the regional youth orchestra, but only slightly. He used to sit in on rehearsals sometimes. The conductor knew Simon and his uncle really well. Simon never missed a chance to point out any errors I made. Even when I didn't make any mistakes, he made sure to tell me that my playing was mediocre. He actually said that. *Mediocre.* Whereas Alicia…" She shook her head angrily.

"I don't know how that note ended up inside that sheet music," she continued. "Maybe Tina dropped it by accident. Or maybe she slid it under her music when Mr. Todd came around. He was always wandering around, looking at what we were doing. She must have forgotten about it. God, I wish I'd never written it. You have to believe me, Riley. For sure no one else will—not now."

I promised to keep on trying to find out what really happened. I even believed her—she seemed too anguished to be lying to me. But, like her, I wished she'd never written that note. It was going to make things a lot harder for her—and for me.

SEVEN

The reminder announcement came over the school PA system the next morning: A memorial service was going to be held for Alicia that evening. Those who knew her were urged to attend.

"I have to go," Ashleigh said at my locker at lunch. "I don't suppose you want to come with me?"

"Sure," I said. I had planned to attend anyway. I pulled a hoodie out of my locker.

"What do you need that for?" Ashleigh asked. "Aren't we going to the cafeteria?"

I had also decided to check out the woods where Alicia's body had been found. The police had already been over the area with a fine-tooth comb and collected whatever evidence there was. What drew me there were the woods themselves. We had been fairly deep into them when Charlie found Alicia, yet no one had thought to look for her there in the first place. Clearly it wasn't somewhere she had been known to frequent, or someone would have pointed that out earlier and looked for her there sooner. It had taken a random sighting by a passing truck driver to alert her parents and the police to this possibility. So what had she been doing there in the first place? Where had she been going?

I told Ashleigh where I was going. "You want to come with me?"

She was shaking her head before I even finished. "No way. There's creepy stuff in there."

"Creepy stuff?" I hadn't considered that. "Like bears?"

"Not lately," she admitted. "But it has happened. Trust me, Riley. There are things in there that are scary. And big. And I don't like being places where I can't tell if something is lurking out of sight, ready to attack me."

I stared incredulously at her. "But you're a country girl."

"Not by choice, believe me. And if you're smart, you'll stay out of there too. A person could get lost."

"I have a compass." I always have a compass with me. It's attached to my key chain, and I know how to use it because Grandpa Jimmy drilled it into my head when I was a little kid. *You can't get anywhere if you don't know which direction to go*, he always said.

Ashleigh held up a hand. "I pass. I'm sorry. I get claustrophobic in all those trees."

"It's creepy and scary and you're going to let me go on my own?"

"Why don't you ask Charlie to go with you? He's all gung ho about her. He's had a crush on her since first grade." The bitterness in her voice surprised me.

"He was in one of the kindergarten skits with her, wasn't he?"

"Yeah, the little weasel. And he knew I didn't have a part. Anyway, he'd love to be the white knight who helps solve Alicia's murder. Why don't you ask him to go with you?"

"Because you're my best friend." I wasn't trying to flatter her. The words just popped out.

Ashleigh grinned. "Yeah?"

"Yeah. So please come with me."

Ashleigh's eyes narrowed. "With great friendship comes great responsibility, is that it?" She pondered the words. "Maybe I'm not ready to be anyone's best friend."

"Please?" I did my best sad-puppy eyes.

"Why do I have the feeling I'm going to regret this?" Ashleigh said. That's when I knew I'd won.

We speed-walked to the woods and, after a compass check, plunged in where we had started on Sunday morning. I was sure I would remember everything and that I would have no problem locating the place where Charlie had found Alicia. In actual fact, it took a lot longer than I'd expected to find the spot, and I recognized it only because of the crime-scene tape, which had come loose in a couple of places and fluttered listlessly in the gentle breeze.

"Now what?" Ashleigh said.

I stood in one spot and turned a slow, full circle. "Where was she going?"

"Or coming from," Ashleigh added. "There's not much around here."

From where Alicia had been found, I searched the ground for any clue as to what direction she had come from. Ashleigh was almost out of sight before I found it—another path.

"This way!" I called.

Ashleigh joined me, and we followed the path until it ended in a massive rock outcropping. I stopped, discouraged. Alicia could have come from any direction to get here. Ashleigh stumbled to a stop behind me.

"If we're going to get back to school before the late bell, we'd better go now," she said.

We'd barely had a chance to look around, but I knew she was right. Reluctantly I turned to go back in the same direction we'd come from. A frantic rustling somewhere nearby froze me. I glanced at Ashleigh, who was standing perfectly still, her eyes the size of dinner plates. She mouthed one word—*bear*—and took a step backward with her arms straight out in front of her as if she were bracing to repel an attack.

I stayed where I was and listened. The rustling stopped for a few seconds and then started again.

"Sounds like a small animal," I said.

"Probably a baby bear. You don't want to get between it and its mama, trust me. Let's get out of here."

She was probably right. I didn't know anything about this place. I nodded reluctantly and started to turn away. That's when I saw it.

Not a bear.

A rabbit.

A rabbit in a snare that cut deep into one of its rear legs. The poor thing was thrashing around, desperately trying to shake off the wire but succeeding only in tightening it even more.

I picked my way toward it, poking and prodding the ground in front of me with a thick piece of windfall in case other snares or traps lay hidden under fall's debris.

"What are you doing?" Ashleigh's voice was tinged with fright. "We should go."

"It's got its leg caught in a snare. Is that even legal around here?"

Ashleigh didn't know. Nor did she seem to want to know.

"We should help it," I said.

I tiptoed toward the scared rabbit, but my presence only seemed to panic it even more. I crouched down to make myself less threatening and talked softly to it. It didn't do any good. I crept the last few feet, knelt beside the rabbit and reached to grab it in both hands. I thought if I could calm it down and stop it from pulling the snare any tighter, I might be able to free it. I still think I could have done that if Ashleigh hadn't screamed.

"It's just a bunny, Ash," I said, glancing over my shoulder.

I froze again. Ashleigh's hands were straight up in the air over her head, and she was staring at the same thing I was—the rifle pointed directly at us.

"Finally caught you!" said the man holding the rifle. I recognized him from the day of the search. He was wearing dirty denim overalls, a plaid flannel shirt, an old hunting hat with its flaps sticking up and away from the ears, and heavy boots. He glowered at us from a heavily bearded face.

"I—I didn't do anything." And, yes, I put my hands up too. "I was going to let this rabbit go."

"Uh-huh." He gestured with the rifle. "Stand up. Slow now."

I stood and backed away from the still-struggling rabbit.

"I've seen you before," I said, hands above my head. "You joined the search party to look for Alicia Allen last Sunday. Your name is Rafe."

"Rafe MacAusland," he said with a curt nod. "You?"

"Riley. And this is Ashleigh."

Ashleigh moaned when I said her name.

He kept his rifle steady on me for another few moments and then slowly lowered it and approached the trapped rabbit. He knelt beside the trap and engulfed the poor creature with one of his massive hands. With the other he released the rabbit's rear leg from the snare. The wire had cut through the skin almost to the bone.

"The little critter is going to need some TLC before he goes his own way again." He tucked the rabbit into a leather bag that hung from one shoulder. The bag jerked once or twice before the rabbit settled down. At least, I hope it settled down.

Tentatively I lowered my hands. Ashleigh kept hers high. Her eyes were glued to the man with the rifle.

"Are you a ranger or a game warden or something like that?" I asked.

The man snorted. "These woods are my front yard and backyard," he said, "and I take it personal when anyone hunts or traps here illegally. I seem to be the only person who does. The so-called police sure don't do much." He spat on the ground.

"Did you know Alicia Allen, the girl who died?" I asked him.

"No."

"But you joined the search party."

"I don't know that rabbit either," he said. "But I still care what happens to it."

"Did you ever see her here in the woods?"

His eyes narrowed. "You sound like the cops. I don't like cops. Useless. Never do a damned thing when I tell them what's going on in here."

"I bet you know these woods pretty well," I said.

"You bet right."

"Do you ever see people in here?"

"Sure. All kinds of people. There's a nature trail that runs through here, marked with blazes. Different times of the year, people do that walk."

I doubted that Alicia had come to the woods that day for a nature walk.

"Is there anything else around here? Any reason people would maybe cut through the woods on their way to somewhere else?"

He snorted. "You're new around here, aren't you?"

I nodded.

"Kids fool around in here all the time. I know. I've seen them. Then there's people who do things like that." He nodded at the snare that had ambushed the rabbit. "The Pines is that way." He jerked his head back over his shoulder. "Get a lot of kids from there exploring these woods every summer, most of them city kids who don't know their asses from their elbows when it comes to being in nature." He shook his head in disgust. "There's at least one lost kid every year, and none of them has the sense to stay put. They all wander around and make it that much harder to find them. I blame the parents for that. The Trading Post is off that way." He jerked his head in another direction. "You go that way"—another jerk of the head—"and you get to Broom's Corners. And off in that direction, you'll eventually get to the farms out on Route 20."

None of these seemed to be likely destinations for Alicia. So what had she been doing out here, especially so close to dusk?

"Can we go now?" Ashleigh asked in a tiny, frightened voice. Her hands were still up over her head. "We're going to be late for school no matter what."

There didn't seem to be much reason to stay. I had to ask Rafe to point me in the right direction to get back. Ashleigh was not impressed. She stalked silently beside me all the way back to school and remained silent when we reported to the office for late slips. When we were about to step into math class, she said, "You owe me."

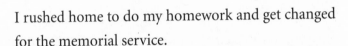

I rushed home to do my homework and get changed for the memorial service.

Aunt Ginny came home earlier than usual. Like me, she was planning to attend. Josh Martin would probably be there too, watching to see who did and didn't attend, checking what people did and what they looked like. She offered me a ride and told me to get a move on because she wanted to be there before the first guests arrived.

I sped through a shower and got changed and was about to head downstairs when I heard voices— a man's and Aunt Ginny's. Rather than interrupt, I waited at the top of the stairs.

"You must be the lady of the house," he said. I imagined Aunt Ginny bristling at the term.

"I pay the rent, if that's what you mean," Aunt Ginny said tartly. She wasn't what I would call a raging feminist, but she sure didn't like being called lady of the house.

The man said he did all kinds of repair and maintenance, and he was looking for work.

"No job is too small, that's my motto," he said.

Aunt Ginny dismissed him with a curt "Thanks, but no thanks" before closing the door firmly and turning to call me. She was pleasantly surprised to see me on the stairs, scrubbed and ready to go.

The memorial service was held in a plush-carpeted, wood-paneled room at a funeral home in town. The parking lot already had a few cars in it when we arrived. Aunt Ginny pulled up to the curb. She did not shut off the car's engine.

"Aren't you coming inside?"

She shook her head. "Got a call from Josh while you were in the shower. I have to go in to work. Call me when you're ready to go home."

I got out of the car and waited near the front door of the funeral home for Ashleigh and Charlie.

Charlie arrived first. He was wearing a suit and a tie.

"You look amazing," I said.

He blushed.

Ashleigh arrived a minute later. She took in Charlie's suit without comment, and the three of us went inside.

A large full-color picture of Alicia sat on an easel at the front of the room beside a lectern. A man in a charcoal-gray suit greeted us at the door. A tasteful brass name tag on his breast pocket identified him as a funeral home employee named Ronald Bishop. He directed us to a guest book sitting on another lectern with yet another photograph of Alicia beside it. Not only was she beautiful, but she was also photogenic. The camera seemed to love her. Charlie signed first and penned a brief message of sympathy to her parents. It turned out to be an excerpt from a poem. Ashleigh read it and groaned.

"What am *I* supposed to write?" she said.

"Just write whatever you feel," Charlie said. "Be sincere."

"Oh, I don't think so." Ashleigh took the pen from him, signed her name and scrawled a brief comment— *With sympathy.* I ended up doing the same thing.

Alicia's parents were standing not far from the door, next to one of the two large photo displays of Alicia. Her father's face was almost a perfect match to the gray of his hair. Heavy bags hung under his eyes, and his black suit looked too large for his gaunt frame. Beside him, his wife stood straight and tall, her mouth tightly set as if she had promised herself she was not going to cry. She wore a simple black dress with black shoes and little gold hoop earrings. Charlie headed toward them. Ashleigh groaned when I started to follow him.

"Do we have to?" She sounded like a whiny six-year-old.

"We have to." Grandpa Jimmy had taught me that. There are times when you have to do things simply because they are the right things to do and not doing them would be hurtful. "Come on."

"I hate this part. I never know what to say."

"Just say you're sorry," I said.

Mrs. Allen took one of Charlie's hands in both of hers and thanked him for coming. A tear formed in the corner of her eye when Charlie said he would never forget hearing Alicia play her violin under the stars the night of her parents' thirty-fifth wedding anniversary. He said it was like an angel making music. Mr. Allen turned away to wipe his own eyes.

Ashleigh nudged me ahead of her.

"I'm very sorry for your loss," I said to the Allens. "I didn't know Alicia very well." Massive understatement. "But I knew her playing, and I know how well liked she was."

"Thanks a bunch," Ashleigh grumbled in my ear.

"I remember you from the search party," Mrs. Allen said, clasping my hand in both of hers. "Thank you for helping."

Ashleigh was next. "I'm sorry for your loss," she said simply. She breathed a huge sigh of relief when we were able to sit down. Charlie wanted to sit up front. Ashleigh refused. I wanted to sit near the back, where I would be able to see everyone. When Charlie refused that too, we compromised by splitting up. Charlie sat up front, and Ashleigh and I sat in the back row near the door, which suited me because it gave me a good view of the whole room and all the people in it.

The room filled up quickly, until it was standing room only. Most of the teachers from school were there.

So were Mrs. Dekes and Mr. Chen. At least half the people there were kids from school, friends of Alicia's. Ronald Bishop moved to the room's double doors and began to close them. He was blocked by the sudden appearance of a tall skinny kid with large bony hands. Simon Phillips, the piano player from school. His ash-blond hair was swept back from his forehead. He was wearing a black suit with a pale blue tie, which made him look even taller and skinnier than usual. He spoke briefly to Mr. Bishop, who then went and whispered in Mr. Allen's ear. Both Mr. and Mrs. Allen turned to look at Simon, but only Mr. Allen followed the man back to the door.

"Mr. Allen, I need the necklace back." Simon's voice was jarringly loud. Mrs. Allen must have heard him, because she turned and looked.

"Necklace?" Mr. Allen looked confused.

"The one I gave her."

Ashleigh leaned in close to me. "I know the one he means. It's gold, I think. It's really beautiful. It looks like some kind of antique. I bet it's expensive."

"Simon, if you could keep your voice down," Mr. Allen said.

Simon obliged, but as close to the door as I was, I had no trouble hearing him. I tried not to be obvious about eavesdropping.

"I really need that necklace back, Mr. Allen," Simon said, his voice more of a stage whisper now.

"I had no idea you'd given Alicia a necklace, Simon."

Mrs. Allen was crossing the room to join her husband.

"Well, I did. I gave it to her a week ago," Simon said.

"He says he gave Alicia a necklace," Mr. Allen explained to his wife.

"Did he?" She looked at Simon. "Did you, Simon? I don't remember Alicia saying anything about it or wearing it. I know it's not in her room, because the police asked me to go through all her jewelry to see if anything was missing. Nothing was."

"No, no, no." Simon shook his head vigorously. "She was wearing it. She wore it every day after I gave it to her."

"I don't think this is the time to be worrying about a necklace, Simon," Mr. Allen said. "Mrs. Allen is upset enough as it is. When we get around to it, we'll see if we can find it."

"No." Simon's loud voice once again attracted the attention of everyone in the room—including his uncle, Mr. Todd. He was in the front row, but he stood up and headed for the back of the room. "You don't understand," Simon said. "It was special. It belonged to my grandmother. She gave it to my mother. I have to get it back."

"I said we'll look for it, Simon, and we will." Mr. Allen looked pleadingly at Mr. Bishop, who touched Simon's arm in an attempt to steer him out of the room.

"She was wearing it. She was wearing it, and I need it back."

Mr. Bishop closed his hand around Simon's arm.

"We're going to start the service now," he said. "If you want to stay, you have to be quiet."

Simon opened his mouth to protest. But before he could speak, Mr. Todd said, "Stop right this minute, Simon. Either go and sit down or go outside and cool off."

Simon spun on one heel and left the room.

"I'm so sorry, Roger," Mr. Todd said to Mr. Allen. "Phyllis, I apologize, but you know how Simon can be."

Mrs. Allen nodded and offered a weak smile.

Mr. Bishop leaned in to Mr. Todd and whispered something. Everyone took their places. I slid out of my seat and chased after Simon.

"Hey," Ashleigh hissed as the door closed behind me.

Simon was at the far end of the thickly carpeted hall. I had to run to catch him.

"Simon?"

He turned and looked down at me. "Do I know you?"

"I go to your school. My name is Riley. The necklace you were talking about—"

"You know where it is?"

"No. No, I'm sorry. You said Alicia was wearing the necklace you gave her. I was just wondering—when was the last time you saw her wearing it?"

"Last week. Before she…before she…" His lower lip began to tremble.

"Did you see her wearing it the day she disappeared?"

He nodded.

"Are you sure?"

"Positive."

"You must have really cared for her," I said slowly. "I mean, if you gave her your grandmother's necklace."

"We were close," Simon said, and for the first time I saw a blaze of emotion other than anger in his face. If you ask me, it was love.

"Are you sure about the last time you saw her, Simon? You didn't see her later? Maybe you lost track of time?"

Suddenly he was furious. "Why are you asking me all these questions? What do you have to do with Alicia? You didn't even know her."

He pushed his way through the door and into the night.

I hurried back into the room where the service was already under way. The room was packed. Tina and Desiree were in the third row from the front. Brendan Mitchell was in the row in front of them. The mayor was there. So were the local member of the provincial legislature and the local Member of Parliament. The chief of police was there in full uniform. I thought it was too bad that Aunt Ginny and Josh Martin weren't there—or any other police officers, for that matter. It seemed a perfect spot to observe and listen and even talk to people.

I slipped into my seat next to Ashleigh and half listened to the tributes to Alicia, starting with her church minister's. He was followed by several of her friends. A girl named Catha, who called Alicia her best friend, spoke, as did a boy named Lomax, whose family was close to the Allens—they were next-door neighbors in cottage country as well as in town. Mrs. Dekes spoke. Mr. Todd spoke. I glanced at Ashleigh halfway through his eulogy.

"Alicia was by far the most talented young violinist that I have ever encountered in my nearly fifty years of life in music. Hers was a natural talent that understood instinctively how to coax exquisite music from her instrument. Her playing would make the angels weep, it was that beautiful. She had so much to give, whether she realized it or not. Not only will I miss her, but the whole world is missing out on an outstanding musical talent."

Ashleigh rolled her eyes. When I looked at her disapprovingly, she was unrepentant.

"The whole world? Give me a break," she hissed.

The final speaker was Mr. Allen. He clasped the podium with both hands, and when he began to talk, he was so overcome by emotion that he had to stop almost immediately. The whole audience held its collective breath, wondering if the poor man was going to break down. Who wouldn't, having lost a child to murder? But he didn't break down. He raised his head slowly, and he painted a picture of the day Alicia was born. Other story pictures followed— Alicia mesmerized by the sound of a violin. Alicia crying, disappointed, after her first attempt to make the violin sing. Alicia's eyes, filled with passion, as she played complex pieces with increasing ease. Alicia in her spare time (What spare time? I wondered), skiing, swimming, lifeguarding at the beach the past summer, laughing with her friends, always laughing, always cheerful, always sunny. Some people sniffled. Some people cried. Almost everyone was red-eyed by the time Mr. Allen had finished.

When it was over, Mr. Bishop invited everyone to step into the room across the hall for light refreshments. Mr. and Mrs. Allen left first, and slowly everyone else stood and shuffled after them.

Tina, I noticed, zipped over to Brendan and started talking to him. They left the room together. Ashleigh and I stood up.

"Now what?" Ashleigh asked.

I glanced around. "Did you see where Charlie went?"

Ashleigh scanned the room. "He probably went for food. Let's go find him. I want to get out of here."

Desiree hurried back into the room and stopped just past the threshold. She seemed to be looking for someone.

"You go look for Charlie," I said to Ashleigh.

She glanced at Desiree, then at me, and shrugged. "We'll be at the refreshments."

I approached Desiree.

"Are you okay? You look a little shaky," I said.

"I'm fine." Her voice was barely audible.

"I saw Carrie yesterday."

Her eyes widened. "You did? Is she okay? I keep trying, but I still can't get through to her."

"She's scared." I let Desiree absorb that. "She thinks the police are convinced she's guilty. Do you think she did it, Desiree? Is Carrie the kind of person who could have killed Alicia?"

"No! Carrie would never do anything like that! Never!"

"What about that note they found in the music room?"

Her eyes shifted away from mine. "I have to go. I have to find Tina."

"I saw her a minute ago. She was with Brendan Mitchell. It didn't look like she was in any hurry to leave."

"She is?" Desiree stepped out into the hall and looked around, as if she didn't believe me.

"Desiree, do you know anything about the note?" I asked again. When she didn't answer, I added, "Carrie is in big trouble. You keep saying you're her friend. If you know something, then you should tell the cops. Carrie could end up in prison. It's no joke."

Tears sprang to Desiree's eyes.

"Desiree?"

"Not here," she said. "Let's go somewhere." She walked quickly down the hall, and I followed her out into the chilly night. Desiree looked around to satisfy herself that we were alone, and even then she kept her voice low.

"You have to warn Carrie about Tina."

"What do you mean?"

She glanced around again.

"Desiree?"

"It's all Tina's fault." She seemed to hold herself straighter once she'd said it, as if a giant weight had been lifted off her.

"What's all Tina's fault?"

"It's true that Carrie was jealous when Alicia got the spot in the national orchestra. Carrie wanted it so badly. She was sure that Mr. Todd lobbied hard to get Alicia the position, and she didn't think it was fair. But she's not a mean person. She's not vindictive. Not like Tina."

My heart revved up when she said that. I waited for her to continue.

"Tina was the one who was always trashing Alicia, not Carrie. Every time Tina saw Alicia, she said something nasty about her. Tina was even more jealous of Alicia than Carrie was. I told you that Alicia and I tutored kids in reading at the library?"

I nodded.

"Well, Alicia tutored Brendan's little brother. Tina used to come to the library to meet up with Alicia after Reading Buddies because Brendan always picks Zak up. Tina has a huge crush on him. And I mean huge. She's done everything but throw herself in the path of his car. Seriously. But so far she hasn't had any luck with him. You want to know why?"

Of course I did.

"Because he's crazy—*was* crazy—about Alicia. You should see the way he looked at her. Tina went nuts the first time she saw them together. And I mean *really* together."

"When was that?"

"Maybe a week or so before Alicia died. Then when Mr. Todd announced a few days later that Alicia had won the spot in the national youth orchestra, you should have heard Tina. She called Alicia *teacher's pet* and said she only got the first violin position because of that and not because she was more talented than Carrie. She kept at it. It was like she was trying to get Carrie all worked up and angry just because she was angry. I guess misery really does love company." She sighed. "Carrie's a good musician. She does really well in all the competitions she enters. Second isn't bad. Second is great. But Carrie always feels like it's first place or nothing. I wish she wasn't so insecure."

She gave me a wary look. "I'm not sure I should tell you." She bit her lip. "It's about her parents."

"Carrie told me her real parents died."

That seemed to take Desiree by surprise.

"She never tells anyone that. I thought Tina and I were the only people who knew." She looked me over as if reappraising me. "She must really trust you."

"She needs someone to believe in her."

"And you do?"

"I don't think she'd ask me to help her if she'd really done it."

Desiree thought this over and nodded.

"Edward is okay, but Marion is horrible. Marion was always boasting about Carrie when she was little. To hear her talk, Carrie was the prettiest, sweetest, most talented little girl who ever lived. Any mom in town will tell you that. I heard my mom talking to one of her friends one time. She said the way Marion went on, you'd think she was the only person in the world with a daughter. But that was when Carrie was little. Marion hasn't bragged about her in a long time. Kids grow up. Then they're not so cute. When they have problems, they're bigger problems. I don't know what Marion said to Carrie, but it must have been something, because by the time we got to high school, Carrie was determined to be the best at everything she did. It was like she had to prove to Marion that she was worthy of being loved."

"Tina had a job last summer doing data entry at the office where Marion works. She says she heard Marion on the phone to Edward one day. She was complaining about Carrie. She told him that if she'd had any idea how Carrie was going to turn out, she never would have agreed to be her guardian, much less tell everyone Carrie was her daughter. She asked why Carrie couldn't have turned out more like Alicia. Tina told Carrie." She sighed.

"Up until then, Carrie and Alicia were friends. They had the same music teacher after school. They were both in the school orchestra and the youth orchestra. They even practiced together sometimes. But all that stopped as soon as Tina told Carrie what she'd heard. Seriously, if Tina had kept her mouth shut, I don't think Carrie would have had such a big problem with Alicia getting the position. But Tina kept running down Alicia, and all of a sudden Carrie saw Alicia as a rival instead of a friend. If you ask me, Tina knew what she was doing. She's the one who had a problem with Alicia, not Carrie. Tina was the one who was really jealous."

"Why are you telling me this, Desiree?"

"Tina and Carrie passed notes back and forth in music class all the time. I saw them. Sure, they were totally juvenile, and I don't doubt Carrie wrote that note the cops found. But Tina wrote notes too. And they were just as bad. Maybe even worse."

"What did they usually do with the notes after class?"

"I don't know. Put them in their pockets, I guess. Or threw them in the garbage."

That's what I would have thought too.

"So how do you think Carrie's note got into some kid's music?"

My thinking was that someone must have put it there, because it sure didn't crawl in there all by itself.

"I don't know."

The note had gone from Carrie's hand to Tina's. It was Tina's to dispose of. Instead of throwing it away or slipping it into her pocket, had she slid it between the pages of a music score? It was the only expla-nation I could think of for how it had gotten there. But why would Tina do that to a friend?

"If you see Carrie again, tell her to be careful of Tina, that's all," Desiree said.

"Do you think Tina could have had anything to do with Alicia's death?"

"Tina?" She looked at me with troubled eyes. "I don't know. I really don't know." She bit her lower lip. "The cops say Carrie doesn't have an alibi. Well, neither does Tina. I texted her that afternoon after school. I had forgotten to write down our English homework assignment. She didn't answer me until late that night."

"Maybe she didn't get the text right away."

She was shaking her head before I finished talking.

"Tina always has her phone on. Always. She checks it constantly. And answers right away. And never with just one text. You text her a simple question and all of a sudden you're in this whole long text conversation with her. But she didn't answer right away that day. I thought maybe her phone was out of power, so I called her house. No one answered. There was no one home."

"Did you ask her about it?"

"She said she took a nap after school."

"You don't believe her?"

"Tina take a nap? Are you kidding? She's practically hyperactive. If she's not texting, she's on Facebook or Instagram. She likes to check up on what everyone else is up to. Especially Brendan."

"Desiree, did the police talk to you about Alicia?"

She nodded.

"Did you tell them what you just told me?"

"No way. I'm not going to accuse Tina of anything unless I'm one hundred percent sure that she did it. And I'm not. She wouldn't do it. She's not a murderer."

"But you think Carrie isn't either."

She hesitated, but finally shook her head. "They're both my friends. I just don't know."

When we rejoined the rest of the guests in the refreshment room, the place was abuzz with whispers. Ashleigh waved at me from the sweets table. She made her way toward us. She was carrying a couple of chocolate-frosted brownies on a paper napkin.

"Where were you?" she demanded. "I looked for you everywhere."

"What's going on?" The buzz was turning into a hubbub. Over by the coffee urns, Mrs. Allen was clinging to Mr. Allen as tears rolled down her cheeks.

"They made an arrest," Ashleigh said.

"Who?"

"Who do you think? Carrie."

EIGHT

Desiree's face turned chalk white.

"Where's Tina?" she asked.

"She left a few minutes ago," Ashleigh said. "With Brendan Mitchell."

"I have to find her." Desiree looked around wildly. "I have to tell her." She hurried away. Ashleigh was ready to go too.

"I talked to the parents. I signed the book. I sat through the speeches. My work here is done," she declared.

"What about Charlie?" I asked.

"He was just here."

I looked around but didn't see him anywhere. I texted him. He was already at home. I called my aunt next. When I told her I was ready to go home, she said she was tied up at work and asked if I could stay overnight with Ashleigh.

"I probably won't be able to get away for hours," she said.

I guessed it had something to do with the arrest.

Ashleigh and I decided to walk to her house.

"So," Ashleigh said, "it looks like Carrie did it after all."

"I'm not so sure about that." I filled her in on everything Desiree had told me.

"What are you saying?" Ashleigh said. "Do you think Tina did it?"

"Tina had a motive," I said. "She was insanely jealous of Alicia, especially when Brendan Mitchell got interested in her."

"You scratch just about any female in school, and you'll find someone who was insanely jealous of Alicia but won't admit it," Ashleigh said. "Who isn't jealous of perfection?"

"As far as we know, you and Tina were the only people who saw the shoving match between Alicia and Carrie. The police knew about it, and since you didn't tell them, Tina must have. Then there's the note. Carrie wrote the note to Tina. Tina was the last person to have it in her hand, yet it conveniently ended up in some sheet music where someone was bound to find it."

"The sheet music is in the music room. It's in big stacks, and everyone takes one when they get to class," Ashleigh said. Unlike me, she took music.

"Tina must have planted that note. She wanted someone to find it."

"You're saying she framed Carrie?"

I was definitely leaning in that direction. "I'm saying that she's as likely a suspect as Carrie is. She was jealous of Alicia. She egged Carrie on. She poisoned Carrie against Alicia."

"I don't suppose she has an alibi for the day Alicia disappeared, does she?"

"Not according to Desiree. And you saw the way she acted while we were out searching for Alicia that morning. She was chattering about fashion! She wasn't paying much attention to what she was supposed to be doing. And from what Desiree told me, she made nasty comments about Alicia all the time. She wanted Carrie to get all worked up just like she was. She wanted an ally against Alicia. And, Ashleigh, both Desiree and Tina know I'm in contact with Carrie, but Desiree is the only one who's asked me how Carrie is doing and who wanted to send a message to her. Tina hasn't approached me at all."

"That sounds like motive to me," Ashleigh said.

"Sounds like? It *is* motive." It was all so clear.

"Did she talk to the cops?"

I nodded. Tina had told me so the first time I spoke to her.

"I bet she told them how Carrie felt about Alicia. But I bet she kept her own feelings to herself," I said. It was obvious. The police had arrested Carrie and left Tina alone. "Tina's alibi isn't any better than Carrie's. She says she was taking a nap."

"So what are you going to do? Talk to your aunt?"

With Carrie under arrest, it was going to take more than guesswork to get Aunt Ginny to look at a different suspect. I was going to have to do better than that. I was going to have to break Tina's alibi.

I tossed and turned all night on the fold-out bed that Ashleigh's father had set up for me. It had nothing to do with the bed, which was surprisingly comfortable. What kept me awake while Ashleigh snored gently in her bed nearby was Carrie and Tina and what Desiree had told me.

Given her past, it wasn't hard to see Carrie as insecure and eager to be liked and admired, to be accepted by her friends if not by her so-called parents. Nor was it hard to imagine her being manipulated by Tina into seeing Alicia as an enemy and an obstacle to achieving what she wanted. But would she have killed Alicia to get her out of the way? And was she scheming enough to beg me for my help if she had really done it? She'd been cooperative too. She had answered all of my questions. She'd volunteered the information about the quarrel with Alicia. She'd admitted to writing the note. She'd confessed her envy of Alicia and attributed her success to favoritism, even though everyone else felt that Alicia was simply the more talented of the two. And what about the day of the search? If she had really killed Alicia, would she have called attention to herself by coming to see why Charlie had stopped? Would she have reacted the way she did, practically going into shock, if she'd been the one who had killed Alicia?

And then there was Tina. Tina who whispered nasty things about Alicia in Carrie's ear all the time. Tina who claimed it was favoritism, not talent, that led to Alicia winning a spot in the national youth orchestra. Tina who had lied to me about telling the police she had witnessed a fight between Carrie and Alicia. Tina who had been the recipient of the damning note written by Carrie. Tina who had not disposed of the note as she usually did, so that *somehow* it had been found and used against Carrie. Tina who had a crush on Brendan Mitchell, who himself had eyes only for Alicia. Tina who had been dogging Brendan ever since. Where exactly had Tina been the day that Alicia disappeared?

I borrowed an outfit from Ashleigh the next morning, which wasn't easy because she's taller than me, with narrower shoulders. She also wears clothes that aren't my style. I ended up in rolled-up jeans and a slouchy powder-blue sweater.

"It looks better on you than it does on me," Ashleigh said as she appraised me.

We had a quick breakfast and left for school. The walk from Ashleigh's house wasn't long. It took ten minutes. I wished that Aunt Ginny had rented a house in town instead of a couple of miles outside of it. It would have made my life easier. We met Charlie on the way. I wished there was some way I could find out where Tina had been the day Alicia disappeared, and I finally said so the third time Charlie asked me what was bothering me.

"It's like you're a million miles away," he said.

"She still thinks Carrie didn't do it." Ashleigh's tone made it clear that she did not share my faith in someone who had just been formally arrested.

"I know Alicia didn't show up for Reading Buddies that afternoon. She had already arranged for a replacement. A permanent replacement, which means she had decided to quit the program. But so far I haven't found anyone who knows why. So if she didn't go to Reading Buddies and she didn't go home, where did she go?"

"Um, to the woods," Ashleigh said, as if I had forgotten.

"What if Tina followed her?"

"Followed her and killed her?"

I nodded grimly and wondered what Aunt Ginny did when she was faced with situations like this. Probably she talked to everyone she could think of, anyone who might have seen the suspect that day. In this case, that would mean every single teacher, student and staff member who was at school that day. That was what she was paid to do. That was what her job and her badge gave her the authority to do. But it wasn't something that I could easily manage. It seemed like an insurmountable obstacle.

I barely paid attention in class all morning. Was I right to believe in Carrie? Was Tina the instigator I believed her to be? How could I find out where she'd gone after school the day Alicia died?

At lunch, I sat in the cafeteria with Ashleigh and poked listlessly at the egg-salad sandwich Ashleigh's mother had kindly made for me.

"Hey, my mom makes the best egg sandwiches ever! And this bread? Omigod, you have to taste it." Ashleigh took a huge bite of hers.

I was lifting my sandwich to my mouth, more out of consideration for Ashleigh and her mom than because I was hungry, when someone shouted my name.

It was Charlie.

He wove like a dancer through the maze of tables and kids.

"Come on." He grabbed me by the arm and started to drag me to my feet. "Come on, hurry up."

"What the—" Ashleigh began.

Charlie, red-faced and covered with a sheen of sweat, was breathing faster than usual. I deduced that he had been in a big rush to find me. Whatever he wanted to show me—and it seemed pretty clear he wanted to show me something—was pretty important.

"It's okay," I said to Ashleigh. "I'll be right back." I glanced at Charlie. "I will be back, right?"

"Yeah, yeah, yeah. Now come on." He grabbed my hand and hustled me out of the cafeteria and through one of the rear exits. He didn't stop when we got outside. If anything, he sped up, moving fast toward the rear of the athletic field. He didn't stop until we reached a gray-haired man in work overalls who was preparing the frame for what I could now see was going to be a walkway that joined the back of the school to the street behind it. A broad, shallow trench had already been dug, and the man was hammering wooden frames into it with a heavy mallet. He paused when he saw Charlie and wiped his brow with the sleeve of his work shirt.

"You back again?" He smiled good-naturedly at Charlie.

"This is my friend Riley," Charlie said between gasps for air. "Riley, this is Mr. Dvorak."

"Riley, huh?" He shook my hand with a firm, dry grip. "Not the famous Riley Donovan who makes headlines in the *Pioneer*." The *Moorebridge Pioneer* is the weekly newspaper. "Pleased to meet you, young lady."

"Tell Riley what you told me." Charlie's eyes were glistening with excitement. He started talking again before Mr. Dvorak could speak. "Mr. Dvorak is working on a walkway. He's been working on it for nearly two weeks."

"Seven school days so far," Mr. Dvorak said.

Seven school days ago was last Wednesday. I looked at him with new interest.

"He was out here after school the day Alicia disappeared." Charlie's whole body thrummed with excitement. He couldn't seem to keep still. "He saw all the kids that came out the back way that day."

Seeing a bunch of kids was one thing. Remembering them all with certainty was another. I looked skeptically at the man. He was in his sixties at the very least. How reliable was his memory? How good was his eyesight?

"Go ahead, Mr. Dvorak," Charlie urged. "Tell her what you saw."

"What part in particular?"

"The part about seeing Tina."

"You saw Tina after school on Wednesday?" I asked.

"I sure did."

"She came out the back way? She went past you?" He nodded again.

"He saw her." Charlie puffed up with pride. "He saw Tina go out the back after school on Wednesday. She could have been headed for the woods, Riley."

"Nah, I don't think so," Mr. Dvorak said.

Charlie stared at him, stunned. I guess he'd been so excited about finding someone who had seen Tina that he had come to get me without asking any more questions.

"Are you sure it was Tina?" I asked.

Mr. Dvorak's eyes twinkled. "Sure I'm sure. I've known Tina most of her life. I've known most of these kids most of their lives. I'm in charge of both the elementary school and the high school, so I see kids from the time they start school until they graduate."

"And you're sure it was last Wednesday?"

He exchanged glances with Charlie before he said, "I'm sure as rain in April. I was out here measuring and setting my stakes, and I saw her."

"But you don't think she was headed for the woods," I said. "How come?"

"Because of what she was doing."

"Which was?"

"She was following someone. She was trying hard to look like she wasn't, but she was. She definitely was."

My heart fluttered. Maybe I was right about Tina after all.

"Did you see who she was following?"

"Sure did. It was the Mitchell boy. Not the little one, but the older one. Brendan."

"Tina was following Brendan Mitchell?" That wasn't the answer I'd expected, and it was no help to me and my theory. Unless..."Was Brendan alone, or was he with someone?" Like, say, Alicia?

"He was with someone."

I felt another surge of excitement.

"Did you see who it was?"

Mr. Dvorak nodded without hesitation. "It was Paul de Villiers."

"Brendan and Paul hang out together," Charlie said.

"That's what I just said, isn't it?" Mr. Dvorak said.

I felt completely deflated. Another dead end.

"Did you see where they went?" Charlie asked.

"Sure did." It was Mr. Dvorak's standard answer. "They cut across the field and through the gap in the fence. They were headed north."

"How can you be so sure they weren't headed to the woods?" I asked.

"Because it was Wednesday. Because Brendan cuts through the back way every Wednesday so he can pick his brother up at the elementary school a couple of blocks over." He nodded toward the north. "Takes him to the library for a reading program. I expect that's where they were headed."

"And Tina followed them all the way?"

"Don't know. Lost track of them once they were through the fence," Mr. Dvorak said.

I thanked him, and he and Charlie chatted for another minute about Charlie's parents and his cousin Rick. I thought about Tina. I brooded about her back in the cafeteria, where I ate the sandwich Mrs. Wainwright had made me. Ashleigh was right. It was the best egg-salad sandwich I had ever tasted. It may have been the paper-thin slices of green onion. Or maybe it was the tiniest whisper of garlic.

"So, dead end with Tina, huh?" Ashleigh said.

I polished off the last bite of sandwich and wiped my hands on a paper napkin. "I need to talk to Brendan," I said.

Ashleigh shook her head. "You're like a dog with a bone. You're not going to let go, are you?"

"Not until I check out Tina's story. I want to hear what Brendan has to say."

"Okay." Something in her tone made me think she was humoring me. "I know where he lives. We can go there after school."

We met up at my locker as usual and Ashleigh led the way. After a few minutes she said, "It's in the next block."

I noted that we were only a few blocks south of the woods where Alicia had been found.

Ashleigh came to an abrupt halt a few seconds later.

"That's Paul de Villiers," she said, pointing to a tall thin boy in jeans and a jean jacket who was raking leaves off an expansive front lawn. "Come on."

Before I could protest, she was standing on Paul's lawn, introducing me and asking after his little sisters, who, it turned out, Ashleigh also babysat.

"You remember last Wednesday, right, Paul?" she asked.

"I remember there was a last Wednesday. Why?"

"Do you remember anything funny when you left school that day?"

"Funny?" He frowned. "What do you mean?"

"You left school with Brendan, didn't you?" I asked.

Paul thought for a moment. "Yeah. I went with him to pick up Zak and walk him to the library."

"Did you notice anyone behind you, anyone following you?" I asked.

Paul stared at me, then at Ashleigh. "What's going on?"

"It's about Alicia," Ashleigh said.

"What about her?"

"Did you see Tina following you on Wednesday after school?" I asked.

Paul's eyes narrowed. "I thought you said it was about Alicia."

"It is."

Paul's frown deepened, but I guess he was curious because he said, "Yeah. I saw Tina."

"Was she following you?"

"Yeah. She was trying to pretend like she wasn't, but she was."

"How long did she follow you guys?"

"Come on," Paul said. "She was following Brendan, not me."

"So you know about her crush on Brendan?"

Paul laughed. "Everybody knows. She stares at him all the time. Did I say stare? I meant drool. But she's wasting her time."

"What do you mean?"

"Brendan had a thing for Alicia. In fact, he looked at her pretty much the same way that Tina looks at Brendan."

"Brendan had a crush on Alicia?"

"Yeah. I kept telling him to go for it, but Brendan isn't that kind of guy. He'd never step on anyone else's toes."

"Whose toes do you mean?"

"That freak Simon. Alicia and Simon were a number. Brendan kept hoping they would break up, but it never happened. I told him to get in there and give it his best shot. Seriously, Brendan's a great guy. And normal. Not like Simon and his creepy uncle."

"Creepy uncle? You mean Mr. Todd?"

"Yeah. Mr. Musical Genius. At least, that's how he likes to present himself. For all I know, maybe he is some kind of genius. I have a tin ear. All that old-fashioned music sounds the same to me. But I've heard how Todd screams at the kids in his class. I went out with a girl who plays flute. She was in tears one time when he humiliated her in front of the class. Said she didn't practice enough. She practiced all the time. It was why we broke up. She never made time for any fun. It got so she was a nervous wreck from practicing, because she didn't want him to scream at her. I don't know how he gets away with it." He paused. "Except that he's supposed to have all this influence, and kids who are serious about their music want to get on his good side so he can write them a recommendation and help them get into a music program when they graduate."

Whoa. I was reeling from all the information he was giving us. But none of it had to do with what I wanted.

"You saw Tina following you. Did she ever catch up to you?"

"Sort of. I saw her, but I don't think Brendan did. We went to get Zak, and we took him to the library, where he freaked out because Alicia wasn't there. He was really upset. We took Zak home. Tina followed us there too. But she went away after we got inside. It wasn't like she was going to ring the bell or anything like that. She was just trying to accidentally on purpose run into Bren."

"Did you see where she went?"

"Nah. I just saw she was gone."

"You didn't see Alicia, did you?"

"If Alicia had been around, Brendan would have found some way to talk to her." He shook his head. "I kind of wish she had been. Maybe she'd still be alive."

"Do you remember what time it was when you noticed Tina was gone?"

"Sure. It was about four thirty."

That left plenty of time for Tina to find Alicia and kill her.

NINE

"It's not Tina," Aunt Ginny said. She was home, but just barely, with heavy bags under her eyes and a grayish tinge to her complexion. I knew she'd had a long night and probably wanted nothing more than to tumble into bed for a few hours' sleep, but I had to tell her what I suspected.

"But Aunt Ginny, she had a motive. She followed Brendan Mitchell, who lives a couple of blocks from the woods. She had plenty of time to kill Alicia. And she doesn't have an alibi."

"It's not Tina. She was at home at the time Alicia was killed."

"That may be what she says, but she's lying. She lied to me more than once, Aunt Ginny. She's like that."

Aunt Ginny flashed me a look of disapproval.

"If you're mixed up in this case somehow, Riley, stop right now."

"But Aunt Ginny, Tina had as much motive for killing Alicia as Carrie did. Maybe more. She was insanely jealous of her. And—"

"I interviewed her neighbors myself. Two different people saw her go into her house a few minutes after five o'clock. That means she couldn't have done it. If that boy is right about the last time he saw Tina, then it means she would have had to get to the woods, bludgeon Alicia to death at five o'clock, get rid of the murder weapon and somehow get home five minutes later."

"Maybe she ran."

"It's a twenty-five-minute walk, Riley. I timed it myself. There's no way she could have done it. In fact, I don't even know why we're discussing this."

"Because Carrie didn't do it."

"And you know this how?"

I didn't dare tell her that Carrie had told me. Aunt Ginny would be furious if she knew I'd been in touch with her. Instead I said, rather lamely, "She doesn't seem like that kind of person."

"No one seems like that kind of person until they actually are." Aunt Ginny's eyes narrowed. "And how do you know what kind of person she is anyway? I thought you didn't know any of those girls."

"I don't. Not really. But Tina is at least as good a suspect as Carrie, and I don't think Carrie did it. What if Tina called or texted Alicia and arranged to meet her in the woods…"

"We have Alicia's cell phone. She didn't make any calls that day, and all the messages she got came in after she was already dead. Her parents called her dozens of times before the cell phone went dead. But there were no calls or message chains at all that day between Alicia and Tina."

"Can't you at least talk to Tina again? You know, interrogate her?"

"Why would I do that? Like I said, there's no way she could have been at the scene on time. End of discussion."

"But—"

"End of discussion, Riley."

"I told you so," Ashleigh said. We had stopped by her house on Friday afternoon after an early closing at school. Ashleigh wanted to get changed before we set off for the library. I had just finished telling her about my conversation with Aunt Ginny.

"I hate to say it again, but I told you so." Ashleigh pulled a sweater over her head. "It was Carrie."

"It wasn't Carrie."

"Why not? Because she says so?"

I didn't feel like talking about it anymore. But that didn't stop Ashleigh.

"Because it sounds like your aunt has done her job. The timing doesn't work. You said it yourself. Alicia was killed at five, but neighbors saw Tina arrive at home a few minutes after five. It seems like a dead end to me."

"Aunt Ginny is assuming that Alicia was killed at five. I think she's assuming that based on Alicia's watch."

"Her watch? I don't get it. What does her watch have to do with it?"

"Aunt Ginny wouldn't tell me. But I'm pretty sure there must have been a struggle, and Alicia's watch got broken. I saw it when I saw the body. I can't think how else she would be so confident about the time."

"The miracle of modern forensic science?"

I shook my head. "That can give you a time range. But for an exact time of death they still rely on things like the last time the victim was seen or things like that."

Ashleigh frowned. "But if her watch was broken when she was killed…" Her eyes widened. She stared at me. "Are you saying the killer changed the time on Alicia's watch to trick the cops?" She frowned again. "But if the watch was broken, how could the killer change the time?"

"She—or he—changed it *before* it was broken."

"Illogical," Ashleigh said. "How do you even see that happening? Tina follows Alicia into the woods…"

"Or lured her into the woods."

"How exactly would she manage that?"

"Maybe she asked to meet her there. Maybe she said she had to talk to her about something."

"In the woods? That doesn't make sense either, Riley."

"If you ask me, nothing makes sense."

Ashleigh ran a brush through her mass of hair. "Come on. Library."

We had a huge history assignment that we wanted to get a start on.

The route from Ashleigh's house to the library took us along wide, tree-lined streets with large square Victorian houses, most of them with gingerbread trim and wraparound porches, sitting on large lawn-covered properties. In several of the yards, people were raking leaves or preparing their flower beds for the coming winter.

"Hey," Ashleigh said. "There's Brendan and Zak." She waved at a tall figure raking the front yard of a yellow-brick house with blue shutters and a bright blue door. A small boy played in the enormous heap of leaves piled in the middle. "Hey, Brendan! Zak!"

Brendan paused and waved back at her.

Ashleigh hurried ahead to greet him. Zak, in a better mood than he had been the last time I saw him, called, "Watch me, Ashleigh!" as he took a running jump into the leaf pile. Ashleigh watched and applauded enthusiastically before turning to Brendan.

"You've met my friend Riley, right?" Ashleigh said. Brendan nodded at me.

"Hi," I said. I don't know why, but I suddenly felt shy, which usually I'm not. Not even remotely. Ashleigh was right. Brendan was hot, and for some reason that intimidated me. Not only that, but he was staring intently at me.

"Ashleigh! Ashleigh!" Zak jumped up and down in the huge heap of red maple, ash and oak leaves. "Come and watch! Come and watch!"

"He's sure feeling better," Ashleigh said to Brendan. "Back in a minute." She jogged across the lawn to Zak. Brendan watched them for a few seconds.

"Tina tells me you're trying to help Carrie," he said finally. "She says you don't think she did it." His large hazel eyes were trained on me.

"And I heard that you and Alicia had recently become an item."

"So?"

"So I was wondering about Alicia and Simon."

"What about them?"

"You heard what happened at the memorial. Do you think he might have been in love with Alicia or obsessed with her?"

"He's a case, isn't he?" Brendan said. "A case of what, I'm not exactly sure. He's like that guy Glenn Gould—you know, the pianist? He was kind of strange. Hummed while he played his music. Called people late at night, and I mean really late at night, to talk to them. Dressed weird. Simon's like that. A little off, you know, but a complete genius at what he does. Alicia said all she ever talked to him about was music, because that was all he ever wanted to talk about. I saw them together all the time. They were always in the music room at lunch or after school. She was at his house all the time. He gave her a neck-lace, and she wore it. They acted like a couple, so I figured they were a couple. Some people confirmed it for me."

I couldn't help asking who had confirmed.

"It was Tina," he said. "She knew Alicia, so I asked her."

"And she said Alicia and Simon were a couple?"

Brendan nodded.

"Is that why it took you so long to ask her out?"

"Yeah. I wish I hadn't waited so long." He cast a glance over his shoulder at his little brother.

"So what happened?" I asked. "What changed your mind?"

His hazel eyes were laced with menace. "And I should tell you this why? So you can help Alicia's killer get off?"

"You really loved her, didn't you, Brendan?"

"She was the nicest, kindest, smartest, most talented, most—" His voice cracked. He brushed away a tear with the back of his hand. "You should have seen her with Zak. She was amazing. Before Alicia, Zak was doing terribly. He was falling behind. My mom worried all the time. Then he joined Alicia's Reading Buddies group, and you wouldn't believe how much progress he's made. She didn't just put in her time and then leave either. She always had great ideas about how to get him reading at home. Every time I went to pick him up, she'd given him a book or had a list of suggestions from the library or a bunch of ideas for games to play with him to make reading and spelling fun. She was a natural. I think that's why she decided to make such a big change in her life."

"What do you mean, a big change?"

"Alicia always had musical ability. That's what she told me, and I know it's true because I've heard her play. Have you?"

I nodded. "But not as a soloist," I added.

"She was unbelievably good. And apparently she was that good at an early age. She was one of those teeny tiny kids carrying a violin case and going to music lessons a couple of times a week. Her parents encouraged her. They encouraged her in everything she did. This tutoring, that was something new, something she only did because you have to put in volunteer hours if you're going to graduate from high school. I finished my volunteering a couple of years ago, but Alicia was always so busy with her music. Back then, if you weren't taking music or in the school orchestra, she didn't know you and you didn't know her. She didn't have time for anything but music. Then she had to get her volunteer hours, and I don't know, I think she really surprised herself."

I still didn't know what he meant.

"She loved it," he told me. "She loved teaching. She said she loved the look in a person's eyes when that person finally made a connection. Like when Zak figured out a new word or when he made his way through a long sentence and then suddenly realized what the string of words he'd just read really meant. She said it was even better than the way she felt when she played a piece perfectly, because when she was teaching someone, it made things better for them instead of just for her. She got all excited about that. She was looking at where she was going to go to school next year. We all are."

I knew from the buzz around school that college applications had to be in by the beginning of January. All the kids who were set to graduate were agonizing over what they were going to do next. If they were going to continue their education, they stressed about what they were going to take and where they were going to go.

"She was going to study music, wasn't she?" That's what everyone had been saying. They said she was a shoo-in for a big scholarship, maybe even one that would pay her whole way.

"That was the original idea," Brendan said. "But she changed her mind. She decided that she wanted to be a teacher. And not a music teacher. She said she wanted to either teach little kids or teach literacy. She hadn't made her mind up about that, but she definitely wanted to be a teacher."

"Nobody mentioned that," I said. "Even her parents seemed to think that she was going to study music."

"That's because she hadn't gotten around to telling them that she'd changed her mind."

"Was she afraid they wouldn't approve?"

"Alicia's parents not approve of something she did?" He shook his head firmly. "They would have done anything for her. If she wanted to be a teacher, they would have done whatever it took to make it happen. They adored her. They had to wait a long time for her to come along, you know. But she hadn't gotten around to telling them."

"Is that why you broke your own rule and asked her out, even though you thought she was with someone else?" I asked. "Because she helped your little brother?"

"I broke my own rule because she was Alicia." A smile tickled his lips. "We were at the library, and we were talking about Zak, and all of a sudden she was asking me about hockey." Like a lot of guys in town, Brendan played hockey regularly, although he wasn't on the professional track. He just did it for fun. "I didn't know that she knew the first thing about hockey, but it turned out that she did. And then—" He shrugged. "Things just kind of took off from there, and the next thing I know, she's telling me about what she wants to do with her life, and it isn't at all what I thought it was." His eyes grew misty, and he looked away from me for a second.

"Did you see her the day that she died, Brendan?"

"I saw her. But I didn't really talk to her. She said she had a million things to do and that she'd tell me about it later that night." His face said what his words left unsaid—she never did tell him, because by the time night rolled around, she was dead.

"Did she give you any details or say where she was going?"

He shook his head.

"She said she would explain later."

I glanced over at Ashleigh, who was lying on the ground, being covered with a crazy quilt of leaves. Zak shrieked as he piled them higher and higher.

"Hey, buddy," Brendan called. "You've got to dig Ashleigh out of there. I have to finish this job and get my homework done."

Zak groaned, but then seemed to have as much fun shoveling the leaves off Ashleigh with his hands as he'd had heaping them onto her.

"Now what?" Ashleigh asked after we had waved our goodbyes.

"The library, like we said." Brendan's information had not gotten me a lot closer to the reason for Alicia being in the woods when she was killed. It did, however, point yet another finger at Tina. It was Tina who had told Brendan that Alicia and Simon were a couple when, in fact, they weren't. It looked as though she had done it to keep Brendan and Alicia apart and, just maybe, give herself a chance at being with Brendan.

We trudged up Brendan's street, one of a half dozen or so in an older subdivision carved from the woods, until we came to the road that ran along the south side of the woods. The few houses that stood on the far side of that road had grassy backyards that ended in scrub and brush, then forest.

Once the houses stopped, there were just trees. Another few minutes and we would make a turn to take us into town and to the library. We were about to make that turn when I saw her.

TEN

She was tall and slender and wearing the same floppy hat I had seen her in at the library, but this time the breeze blew back the brim and I saw her face clearly as she stepped off the road and crossed the deep, wide ditch. There was something familiar about her, but I couldn't place her. She quickly raised a hand to pull the hat brim down again and continued on with her head bowed, one shoulder weighed down by an enormous tote.

"That's the woman from the library," I said. "The one who dropped off the drawing her little boy made, remember?"

Ashleigh stumbled to a stop by my side and did not look up from her phone, which she was busy checking messages. "What? What happened?"

"That woman." I pointed.

She was making fast progress, striding forward in grasses up to her knees. At the rate she was going, she would soon be deep among the trees. I sprinted to catch up with her before she disappeared.

"Hey!" Ashleigh shouted.

The woman had vanished by the time I reached the tree line. I stopped, bent over, gasping for breath and searching for some sign of a trail.

Crack!

The sound came from my left somewhere up ahead. I searched the ground in that direction. It took a minute or two, because the terrain was both rocky and littered with layers of fallen leaves, but I spotted it. A path. I was sure of it. I hurried down it, glancing at my footing and then at the terrain up ahead, scanning for any sign of the woman. Her clothes had all been in earth tones—tan pants, a knee-length brown overcoat, a muddy-brown hat. Nothing that would be easy to spot in the middle of a dense forest, made dark and shadowy by the sun's near-total failure to penetrate the thick canopy overhead. All I could do was stay on the path and keep moving as fast as possible in the hope of overtaking her.

The trees ended all of a sudden, and I stopped in the middle of a large meadow with plants and grasses rising as high as my thigh. There was no sign of the woman. My confidence in my ability to find her started to waver. It took me longer than I would have liked to find the path on the other side of the clearing. By the time I did, Ashleigh, much to my astonishment, had managed to catch up to me.

"What's going on?" She sounded annoyed and not the least bit winded. "What are you doing?"

"I saw that woman, the one from the library, the one in the floppy hat."

Ashleigh stood, one hand on her hip, regarding me with barely contained exasperation.

"What woman? What are you talking about?"

"I don't want to lose her," I said, even though, in all likelihood, I'd already lost her. "Come on."

Ashleigh didn't budge. "What woman?"

"I saw a woman at the library. She was wearing a floppy hat, so I couldn't see her face. She had just dropped off a picture her son had drawn for Alicia.

Her son used to go to Alicia's reading group at the library, and he adored her."

Ashleigh rolled her eyes. "I swear, if I hear about one more person who adored the ever-perfect Alicia Allen, I am going to—"

"I just saw her again, Ashleigh. Going into the woods."

"Uh-huh." She was not impressed. "And?"

"What if that's where Alicia was going the day she died? To see that woman and her son?"

A frown appeared and deepened as Ashleigh considered this possibility. "That's kind of a stretch, don't you think? Just because a woman happens to walk through the woods—"

"A woman who knew Alicia. A woman who had a small boy who was in Alicia's reading group. A woman who cared enough to drop off a drawing at the library for Alicia. Maybe she knows something, Ashleigh."

"If she knew anything, she would have told the police by now."

"Maybe," I said. "I want to find out."

Ashleigh rolled her eyes again but didn't argue with me. We followed the path the woman had taken—

at least, I hoped we were on the right path—for another ten minutes, then another five more.

"I don't suppose you know where we're going?" I asked Ashleigh. After all, she had grown up around here.

"I told you, I don't like woods." She was glancing around obsessively, like a nervous burglar afraid he was being watched by police. "There are too many creepy, not to mention scary, things in here."

I thought about Rafe and his hunting rifle, and the rabbit with its left leg caught in that snare. She wasn't far wrong.

We walked for another ten minutes, by which time Ashleigh was saying over and over, "We should go back. We have to go back. It's going to get dark. We have to get back before it gets dark."

"It's just after four. We have plenty of time. Sunset isn't until quarter past six." How do I know these things? I hear them from Aunt Ginny every day. Her rule when I'm out on my bike, which is pretty much my main way of getting around since we live a mile and a half out of town, is that I have to be home before sunset, whenever that is.

We kept going, with Ashleigh grumbling the whole way, until the woods finally ended at a road.

"Broom's Corners," I said, taking in the hamlet I had visited exactly once before. The woman, of course, was nowhere in sight.

"I hate to ask, but now what?" Ashleigh asked.

"She has to be here somewhere." It only stood to reason.

"What are we going to do? Go door to door, asking to speak to the woman in the floppy hat?"

It wasn't a terrible idea. It's not as if there were hundreds of doors to knock on.

We crossed the road and made our way to the antiques store, where a woman in late middle age appeared to be locking up for the day. Ashleigh stared pointedly at her before looking at the sun, which was already beginning its descent toward the horizon.

"Excuse me, but did you see a lady with a floppy hat go by here?" I asked.

The woman finished locking up the store before she turned to fix me with icy eyes behind powerful bifocals.

"No, I did not," she said sharply. "And even if I had, why on earth would I tell you? Really, a person used to be able to enjoy her privacy around here. Now it's people coming right to your door, asking for work, or approaching you in the street like this.

Complete strangers, asking you questions about people." She shook her head in disgust. "A person used to be able to live a quiet, undisturbed life, unbothered by invasive questions."

"She could have just said no," Ashleigh grumbled as we walked away. "That's the first time we ever talked to her."

We wandered around the Corners, looking for the woman. I even knocked on the doors of a few of the hamlet's houses to ask about her. My cover story was that she had dropped something and I was trying to return it to her. I showed an envelope from my backpack that I had stuffed with a couple of sheets of blank paper.

"People around here are really unfriendly," Ashleigh said after we had been sent on our way by yet another annoyed resident of Broom's Corners.

"They sure don't seem to like people asking about their business," I said. "I guess that's why they live here. They value their privacy."

"Yeah? Well, they're welcome to it. What a bunch of sourpusses." She looked up at the darkening sky and asked her inevitable question. "Now what? How are we supposed to get home?"

It was too dark to navigate the woods again, and it was too far via the long way along the road that ringed the forest. I did the only thing I could think of—I called Aunt Ginny.

"What in heaven's name are you doing in Broom's Corners?" she asked.

I dodged the question and hoped she wouldn't notice. "Can you come and get us? Please?"

I heard a long sigh at the other end of our connection. "Give me thirty minutes."

"Thirty minutes?" Ashleigh groaned. "What are we supposed to do in the meantime?"

I had the perfect idea.

The bakery was small but warm and brightly lit, and it smelled alluringly of freshly baked bread. Its display case was filled with cookies and pastries— bear claws, éclairs, custard tarts, cookies, four different types of squares and some apple-crumble pies.

"Treats are on me," I announced. It seemed the least I could do.

Ashleigh trailed a hand along the display case as she contemplated her choice before finally settling on a white-chocolate-and-macadamia-nut cookie the size of a tea saucer and a mug of hot chocolate.

She settled herself at one of three small tables and lost herself in the contents of her phone as she sipped and nibbled.

I examined the display case to make my choice. While I was trying to decide between a lemon tart and an empire cookie, I heard a small voice, slightly cartoonish—the voice of a young child. What really caught my attention was what it said. I was pretty sure I'd heard the name Alicia.

I ducked behind the counter and peeked through the door into the kitchen. A little boy not much older than Brendan's brother Zak stood in the large, spotless kitchen. A woman knelt on the floor in front of him. It was the woman I had followed. I was sure of it. And no wonder she had looked vaguely familiar. I had seen her before, right here in this bakery, when Charlie and Ashleigh and I had come here on our bikes to hand out *Have You Seen This Girl?* flyers. The woman was trying to comfort the boy.

"Your son knew Alicia," I said quietly.

The woman jumped to her feet and pulled the boy protectively to her.

"Go downstairs, Teddy. Mommy will be there in a minute."

Teddy didn't go. He clung to his mother, presenting her with the chore of disentangling herself and shooing him down the stairs with a promise that she would be there in a minute.

"I saw you at the library," I said. "You were dropping off a drawing your son made. He liked Alicia, didn't he?" The woman stared mutely at me. "Did Alicia ever come here?" I asked.

The woman didn't answer.

"Did she come through the woods to get here?"

"What do you want?" she asked.

"Was Alicia here last Wednesday?"

The woman stared at me. "Please leave."

"You remember me, don't you?" I asked. "I was here before she was found. I was distributing flyers."

The woman looked blankly at me. She clearly didn't remember me.

"The police have been trying to find out what Alicia was doing before she disappeared," I said. "Did she come here?"

"Please." The woman glanced around nervously, as if she was afraid of being overheard. "I don't know anything."

"Did you talk to the police? Did you tell them you knew her?"

The woman fidgeted nervously with her apron. "Please, I don't know anything. You have to go."

"If Alicia was here that day, the police will want to talk to you. And to your son."

The woman's eyes turned steely. "I'll deny anything you say."

"Mrs. Burns can confirm that you and your son knew Alicia. And my aunt is a police detective. She'll believe me. It's a murder investigation. She'll take you in for questioning if you don't cooperate."

The woman's face turned as white as the flour that covered the wooden countertop at her elbow. She stared at me until the silence between us was broken by the jingle of the bell over the bakery door, announcing a customer. But she didn't go out to the front of the store. Instead, she pressed a button on the wall. A moment later an older woman appeared from somewhere behind the kitchen. She bustled through to the front to greet the newcomer.

"Please," the woman said. "Don't make me talk to the police."

It never sounds good when someone wants to avoid the police. It usually means they have something to hide.

"If Alicia was here the day she died, you have to talk to the police," I said.

The woman cast a worried glance at the bakery's front door. She crossed the kitchen quickly and held open the screen door to the back porch. I took the hint and stepped outside. She led me far enough away that we wouldn't be overheard.

"You can't tell anyone what I tell you, not even the police." When I started to protest, the woman cut me off. "Either you promise not to say anything to the police or I tell you nothing."

I studied her face. She was young, not more than thirty, but her face was thin and lined. If I had to name the dominant emotion in her face, I would say it was fear.

"Okay. I promise," I said.

She was still for a moment, except for her hands, which she kept wringing.

"Alicia was supposed to come here after school on Wednesday," she said at last. "She'd been coming twice a week for a couple of weeks. Teddy adored her."

She glanced at me. "Maybe I should back up a little. We met Alicia at the library. I took Teddy there one day. I don't know what I was thinking. There's no way I could get a library card. But Teddy was so lonely for kids his own age. And there was a bunch of kids there with Alicia. She was reading with them, and the children all seemed to be having fun, so I let Teddy join the group. Afterward Alicia came to talk to me. She said she would help me pick some books for him. She even tried to sign me up for a library card."

"I don't understand," I said. "Library cards are easy to get. And they're free for kids under twelve."

She knotted and unknotted the edges of her apron. She glanced nervously at the rear door to the bakery.

"It's my husband," she said. "I can't let him find us. Ever. If he finds me, he'll kill me. I don't know what he'll do to Teddy. I thought we could just take off and start over and he'd leave us alone. I should have known better."

"He's looking for you?"

She nodded, and her face turned hard and bitter.

"He found us once already. He almost killed me. The cops arrested him. He was charged with assault.

Got a month, which they allowed him to serve on weekends because he's such an upstanding citizen. I know he's looking for us. He won't give up until he finds us."

"Can't you get a restraining order?" I asked.

"They won't work with him. He's smart. He's a lawyer. Crown attorney. He's like this with cops." She held out a hand with its index and middle fingers tightly crossed. "Alicia figured it out. That's when she offered to tutor Teddy. I tried to say no. The fewer people who know us, the better."

"Everything okay, Jennifer?" a voice called. The other woman from the bakery was standing on the back porch, regarding us with some concern.

"Everything's fine, Marjorie," Jennifer replied. I doubted very much that Jennifer was her real name, not if she was hiding out in fear for her life.

The woman watched us for another few seconds. "I'm going to need you inside in a few minutes."

"I'll be right there."

Marjorie went back inside.

"She's amazing. All the people here are. They're protecting me."

"Tell me about Alicia," I prompted.

"She started coming here after school. Teddy and I would meet her at the edge of the woods. She was wonderful with him. And she enjoyed herself. She told me she had no idea that teaching children could be so rewarding. Apparently she spent most of her time on music. Violin, I think. Anyway, she didn't show up last Wednesday. I figured something must have come up. It never occurred to me that she had been murdered. I was shocked."

"But not shocked enough to call the police," I said gently.

"What good would it have done? She was killed before she got here. It has nothing to do with me." Her face flushed. "I didn't mean that the way it sounded. I thought the world of Alicia. I'm sorry she died. Believe me, if I knew anything that would help, I'd tell you. But I don't. Please don't tell anyone about Teddy and me. Please?" She glanced nervously at the bakery. "I really have to get back to work."

I followed her inside, where I found Aunt Ginny at the display counter, watching with greedy eyes as Marjorie filled a cardboard pastry box with Aunt Ginny's delicious choices. She ate a custard tart on the way back to town.

ELEVEN

It was a bright, crisp day, the kind of fall day where you smell the tang of the decaying leaves carpeting the ground, and, for the first time since the winter before, your breath plumes out in front of you when you breathe or speak. Or when you huff and puff as you ride your bike into town, which is what I did late Saturday morning. Ashleigh had only a half shift at the supermarket where she worked, and I was meeting her back at her house.

"I'm beginning to think I should have rented a house in town," Aunt Ginny said as I hunted for my gloves. "What are you going to do in the winter?"

"I'll walk." It was just under two miles. At most it would take me half an hour.

"In the snow? On a road with no sidewalks? When you're coming home from school at dusk?" Aunt Ginny shook her head. "I don't think so. I'll have to sign you up for the school bus."

I groaned. The school bus would mean dashing out of school as soon as the bell rang to avoid being left behind in the parking lot. I wouldn't be able to stay to hang out with my friends unless Aunt Ginny was able to pick me up or someone's parents could give me a lift. There had to be another way. I didn't want to lose my freedom the first time it snowed.

I locked up my bike at the side of the Wainwrights' house and was cutting across their rolling lawn when a man came down off the porch, head lowered as he jotted something in the small notebook he was carrying. When he got to the sidewalk, he headed for the house next door. He glanced at me but didn't seem to recognize me. He marched up the front walk of Ashleigh's neighbors and rang the doorbell. I did the same thing at Ashleigh's house. While I waited for an answer, I heard the man ask to speak to the lady of the house.

"What was he doing here?" I asked after Ashleigh ushered me into her foyer.

"Who?"

"That man I just saw on your porch."

"Oh. He's looking for work. I've seen him around. He goes door to door, asking people if they have any odd jobs that need doing. I think he did some work for the Slocums up the street. Why?"

"He's the caretaker at the Pines." I remembered him from when we were posting *Have You Seen This Girl?* flyers.

"I guess he doesn't have enough to keep him busy out there. You want a blueberry muffin? My mom just made them. They're still warm."

"Did you talk to him?" I asked.

"Who?"

"The man who was just here."

She shook her head. "He asked to speak to the lady of the house. I let my mom handle it."

That sounded just like the man who had knocked on our door and spoken to Aunt Ginny. He'd used the word *lady* on the wrong person that day.

I wheeled around and went back out the front door, groping in my pocket for my phone.

"Hey, where are you going?"

I ran down the porch steps and looked up the street. There was no sign of him. Where had he gone? Was he inside the neighbors' house? If he was, he would have to come out soon.

"Mind telling me what we're waiting for?" Ashleigh asked when she joined me on the sidewalk.

"I want to get a picture of that man."

"The handyman? What for?"

"His name is Gord Cooper. At least, that's what he told me."

"At least?"

"He's new around here. I'm sure of it." I had thought long and hard about a turn of phrase he'd used—*from what I hear, no one comes here this time of year except by accident.* He wouldn't have said it that way if he were speaking from experience. "And he's been going door to door, asking to speak to the lady of the house."

"Okay. And…?"

"What if he's not really looking for odd jobs to do?" I said slowly. "What if he's looking for someone? A woman?"

Ashleigh's expression went from puzzlement to a glimmer of understanding.

"Are you saying—?"

"What if he's looking for his wife? And what if he knows that she and his son are somewhere around here, Ashleigh? She said he found her once before. What if he thinks he's close to finding her again, but so far he hasn't had any luck? You saw how that woman at the antiques store reacted when we asked her if she'd seen a woman. It wasn't the first time she'd been asked something like that. And Marjorie at the bakery is definitely protecting her. But what if he somehow found out that Alicia was tutoring his son?"

"You think *he's* Jennifer's husband?"

"What if he followed Alicia? What if he tried to get her to tell him where Jennifer is hiding and she refused, and he killed her?"

"You can't be serious," Ashleigh said. "It's not enough that everyone thinks Alicia was an angel. Now you want to turn her into a saint who died protecting a woman and a child from some maniac?"

But if Carrie hadn't killed Alicia, someone else had.

And if Gord Cooper wasn't who he said he was, I could be onto something.

"We have to get a picture of him. I want to show it to Jennifer. I want to know if Gord Cooper is her husband."

"Even if he is, that doesn't necessarily mean he killed Alicia," Ashleigh said.

"Maybe. But we still have to warn Jennifer." I ran for my bike. "Come on," I called over my shoulder.

Ashleigh had to dash back to lock the house. She grabbed her helmet, jumped on her bike and followed me.

"Where are we going?" she asked between gasps.

"If we see Cooper, I'll take his picture. If not, we go to the Pines."

Ashleigh groaned. "Do you know how far that is?"

"A couple of miles."

"What if he's there when we get there?"

"We take his picture."

"And if he isn't there?"

"We see what else we can find out."

We didn't spot Gord Cooper on our way out of town, nor did any cars or trucks pass us on the way to the Pines. It didn't surprise me, then, when we finally reached the red-roofed cabins of the Pines and didn't see a vehicle anywhere on the property.

"So what's the plan, Stan?" Ashleigh whispered. She dismounted her bike and looked around warily.

"I'm going to check the office. If he's here, I take his picture."

"Just like that?"

"I'll think up some excuse."

"And he won't be suspicious? Especially if he turns out to be who you think he is."

Her negativity was getting me down.

"Do you have a better idea?"

"Actually, I do," she said. "You go and take his picture, and I'll wait here. If you're right about him, and if he tries to kill you, I'll call for help."

"Very funny."

"I'm not joking."

"I'll ask to use his phone. I'll say mine is out of power. I think I can take his picture without him noticing."

"Great. I'll wait here."

I set my bike on its kickstand and headed for the office, leaving her on the driveway.

The door was locked. I peered in through the window. The place looked deserted. I circled the building to see if there was another door or if any windows had been left open. No luck. By the time I got back to the front, Ashleigh was gone, and my cell phone pinged. It was a text. From Ashleigh. **CABIN 12**.

I followed a graveled path to the cabins behind the office. They were arranged in two broad arcs. Cabin 12 was to the extreme right. Ashleigh's bike was leaning against one side of it, out of view of the office, and Ashleigh was standing in its open door.

"It's his."

"Did he leave it unlocked?" I asked.

"As good as." She held up her bank card. "The locks on these cabins are pathetic. If the Big Bad Wolf came along and huffed and puffed…" She stood aside to let me pass. "I don't think you're going to need that picture."

I stood in the open doorway and gazed at the cabin's interior. More precisely, I was transfixed by the wall opposite the end of the bed. It was plastered with photographs—of a woman and a small boy. In all but one of them, the woman's figure had been either blacked out or smeared with red paint—at

least, I assumed it was paint. The one exception was
the largest of the photos, blown up to the point that
it had become pixelated. In that one, a knife pierced
the woman's heart, its point buried deep in the cabin
wall behind it. The woman in the photo had blond
hair, not brown, and her face was fuller, less angular
than now, but there was no mistaking those watchful
eyes, the tentative smile on those bow-shaped lips,
that long, slender nose. It was Jennifer.

"It looks like you were right about him," Ashleigh
said. "Do you think he—"

I shushed her. What was that quick dull *clunk*?
A car door?

I waited, holding my breath. Was he back?

Ashleigh opened her mouth to speak. I held up a
hand to silence her.

"What?" Ashleigh hissed. "What's going—"

I clamped a hand over her mouth and waited for
a few seconds, straining to listen.

"I thought I heard something." Still uneasy,
I stepped into the cabin and took a closer look at
the wall of photos. In a few of them—not many,
but enough—Cooper appeared along with Jennifer.
Most, though, appeared to have been taken by him.

There it was again. A *clunk*, followed by a voice. "Hello? Hel-lo?"

I had left my bike in the driveway near the office. He knew someone was here.

"Take pictures of him," I said. "Quick! Then call my aunt Ginny. Tell her where we are. Tell her what's happening."

"What about you?" Ashleigh said.

"Just do what I said." I shoved her inside the cabin and pulled the door shut.

Cooper came around the side of the office. His eyes zeroed in on me immediately. "Hey, you!" he shouted. "What are you doing there?"

He scowled at me, and for a split second our eyes locked. Then I took off for the woods at a dead run, leading him away from Ashleigh so that she could call the cops. With luck, I hoped to lose him in the trees.

I ran as fast as I could, my eyes focused on the ground so my feet wouldn't tangle with a tree root. Cooper thundered after me. I swear I felt the earth tremble. Or maybe it was my body shaking to the beat of my hammering heart.

I ran. I wasn't following a path. I was just running away from the Pines as fast as I could. I glanced back over my shoulder. Cooper was gaining on me. He was close enough that I caught the look of grim determination on his face. Fighting panic—maybe acting as a decoy wasn't such a good idea after all—I turned forward again and saw the trunk of a fallen hemlock. I raced toward it, jumped and cleared it with no problem—until I landed. The ground on the other side of the fallen tree sloped downward, and I lost my balance. When I tried to compensate, I felt a sharp twinge in one ankle. I crashed to the forest floor. Everything switched to slow motion after that.

I hit the ground hard. Cooper was close enough for me to see the cruel grin of satisfaction on his lips. I tried to get to my feet. Cooper's hand came up. He was holding a gun. It was pointed at me. My brain screamed, *Run!* But my feet refused to cooperate. The barrel of the gun loomed as large as a cannon. Behind it was a pair of hard, hateful eyes. I scrabbled backward on my hands and one good foot, like a three-legged crab. Cooper took aim.

BLAM!

BLAM!

I opened my eyes. Cooper lay spread-eagle on his back in a bed of moss and dead leaves. Ten yards away, Rafe lowered his shotgun. He crunched slowly through the shag of autumn leaves, his eyes steady on Cooper.

"You okay, young lady?" he said without looking at me.

"Yeah. Yeah, I guess." I was trembling all over, even in my hoodie and jacket. My eyes kept going back to Cooper, his chest slick and red with blood, his arms outstretched. I scanned the ground around him.

"He had a gun." Rafe's voice was grim, all business. "I see it."

When he got to Cooper, the first thing he did was pick up Cooper's gun with the filthiest cotton handkerchief I had ever seen. He dropped it into the same leather bag he had used for the snared rabbit. "For safekeeping," he said.

He knelt beside Cooper and pressed two fingers to the side of his neck.

"Is he st-still alive?" My teeth were chattering like a pair of wind-up dentures.

Rafe shook his head. He got to his feet and peeled off his knee-length leather coat and draped it around my shoulders.

"You got a phone with you, young lady?"

As if on cue, my phone buzzed, signaling a text message. **Where r u?**

"Guess you better call someone."

I called Ashleigh, who was breathless.

"I heard shots. Did you hear shots? I swear I heard shots."

"Did you call Aunt Ginny?"

"Yeah. She's really hard to talk to, do you know that?" Ashleigh said. "It was like she was mad at me or something. She kept asking me how did I know everything."

"Is she coming or isn't she, Ashleigh?"

I guess I was a little abrupt, because when Ashleigh spoke again, I heard surprise and hurt in her voice. "Yes. And she wants to know where you are."

I looked up at Rafe. "How do I give directions to here?"

"From where?"

"The Pines."

"We're southeast of there, maybe half a mile."

I relayed the information to Ashleigh.

"Why don't you just come back here?" Ashleigh asked. "And who are you talking to? What happened?"

"I have to stay here. I'll explain later."

"But your aunt is coming *here*." She sounded nervous. She still didn't know Aunt Ginny well. Most of the time, all she saw was stern cop.

"Tell her I can explain, and she'll leave you alone," I said.

"Okay." One word, laced with doubt.

I struggled to my feet and gingerly put a little weight on my hurt ankle. Then a little more. It still hurt, and I was probably going to have a mammoth bruise, but I could walk on it. I sat on a rock away from Cooper and waited. Rafe stood nearby, one leathery hand wrapped around the barrel of his rifle. He didn't say a word. Didn't ask a single question. Until he heard someone crunching and crackling toward us from a northerly direction.

"That'll be the police." He still didn't move. He just waited patiently for Aunt Ginny to appear, which she did, a tiny version of herself in the distance, a flash of her navy jacket, her face, a hand.

"Riley! Answer me if you can!"

"Over here, Aunt Ginny!" I called. "Over here!" I waved my hands over my head to give her a visual.

She appeared fully a moment later, her gun drawn and clasped in both hands, her eyes going first to Rafe and his rifle, and then to Cooper on the ground.

"Ashleigh said she heard shots." Her eyes were on Rafe as she said this. When he started to reach into his bag, Aunt Ginny tensed and raised her weapon.

"He's okay, Aunt Ginny," I said quickly. "That's Rafe. He saved my life."

Aunt Ginny's eyes snapped back to me. She reached in her pocket for her phone and placed a call. Then she turned to Rafe and held out her hand. He plunged his rag-wrapped hand into the leather pouch and brought out Cooper's gun. He passed it butt end first to Aunt Ginny, still wrapped in the raggedy handkerchief. Aunt Ginny nodded. She asked Rafe to stay until more police officers came. He went to lean against a rock outcropping a few yards away. Aunt Ginny came and stood in front of me.

"Why don't you tell me what this is all about?"

I told her everything, including my theory about Gord Cooper as a prime suspect in Alicia's murder. She listened without interruption, but her pinched frown gathered in more and more of her face as I talked, until she was all pointy-faced.

"That man had a gun," she said. "He could have killed you."

"I know, but—"

"You can't do things like that, Riley."

More cops arrived, led by Josh Martin.

"You stay put," Aunt Ginny said. "We'll talk later." She went to meet Josh and fill him in on what had happened.

TWELVE

"So we figured that the husband found out that Alicia was tutoring his son," Ashleigh said to Charlie. She had texted him from the back of the squad car that drove us to the police station to make formal statements. He was waiting for us when we were finally let go, and we'd walked to Ashleigh's house, which was the closest. Aunt Ginny was going to be tied up for a while. Either she would pick me up later or I would spend the night at Ashleigh's again. Jennifer was brought in before Ashleigh and I were told we could leave. I didn't see her, but I did see one of the uniforms doing his best to amuse Teddy.

Ashleigh was relishing her tale. "And then we figured out—"

"*We* figured out?" I hated to interrupt, but...

Charlie grinned. Ashleigh ignored me.

"Alicia was supposed to tutor the kid the day she died, but she never showed up. We figure Cooper must have killed her when she refused to tell him where his wife was hiding. Because he'd been looking for her, Charlie. We figured that's why he was going door to door asking to speak to the lady of the house. He was looking for his wife. He followed Alicia and tried to force her to tell him where his wife was. She refused. He killed her."

Charlie frowned. "Why would he do that? Why kill her? The way you have it figured, Cooper knew that Alicia knew where his wife was, and he killed her trying to find out, right?"

Ashleigh nodded.

"Well," Charlie continued, "leaving aside the question of how he knew that when no one else did, not even her parents or her boyfriend, why would he have killed her? If he wanted to find his wife, why didn't he just follow her instead? She would have led him straight to her."

It was an excellent question, but Ashleigh brushed it aside.

"The man has assaulted his wife. More than once. She's terrified of him. For sure he has anger-management issues. Guys like that always do. He lost his temper when Alicia refused to tell him, and he did what he did to his wife—he beat her. That's how she died, Charlie. She was beaten over the head."

Charlie blanched when she said that, and I kicked Ashleigh under the table. Charlie had found her. If he was anything like me, he'd been having trouble getting the picture of her out of his mind.

"Anyway," she said in a much softer voice, "the cops think he did it. They think he killed Alicia." She looked to me for backup. "Isn't that right, Riley?"

I knew Detective Martin was leaning toward that theory. Aunt Ginny hadn't given away anything. Nor was she likely to tell me much. She was still angry with me.

"We won't know until they make a statement to the media, I guess," I said.

We talked for another half hour or so, jumping from topic to topic and time period to time period—Alicia, kindergarten, school concerts, Carrie, parents and their expectations, how crazy it seemed now that anyone had thought Carrie killed Alicia over a spot in a youth orchestra. Charlie talked about how hard it was going to be for Carrie to return to school and find out who had believed in her and who hadn't.

"That's the worst," Charlie said. He spoke from personal experience—he'd been accused of murder a while back. "One of her best friends did nothing to help her and actually went out of her way to make her look bad." He meant Tina. "I bet that really hurt."

Ashleigh's doorbell rang. It was Aunt Ginny, come to take me home.

"That was fast," I said when I got into the car with her.

She didn't say anything. She stayed silent until I got up the nerve to say something.

"Did you close the case, Aunt Ginny?"

"We spoke to the wife. The husband, whose real name is Brad Donnelly, has a history of domestic violence, that's for sure. He was an officer of the courts, and look how he treated his own wife. He was out on parole. She had a restraining order and the conditions were strict—no contact with his wife or son, not to be within five hundred yards of his wife or son, no alcohol, no firearms."

"That didn't do much good."

"We talked to the PI he hired who tracked the wife down to this general area. Once Donnelly had that information, he apparently took a leave of absence from work to come up here to look for her. She says he always had guns around the house. He liked to use them to threaten her. That's his thing. Guns."

A picture flashed before my eyes—Donnelly's gun, its barrel gaping like the jaws of hell, aimed straight at me. I started to shake.

Aunt Ginny glanced at me. "Are you all right? You just turned as white as a sheet. Is your ankle bothering you? We'll ice it as soon as we get home, just to be on the safe side. Unless you think you want to go to Emerg and get it checked out. Do you?"

I rotated my sore ankle gingerly.

"It hurts, but it's definitely not broken. Let's go home, Aunt Ginny."

For a change, Aunt Ginny was the one who wrestled the leftovers out of the fridge and heated some up for me. She insisted on helping me up the stairs to my room, even though I didn't need help.

"Let me know if the pain gets bad," she said as she closed my door.

I lay in the dark, staring at the ceiling, afraid to close my eyes because every time I did I saw the barrel of the gun again. Cooper—Donnelly—had come after me with a gun. He'd threatened his wife with a gun too. So why had he killed Alicia with a tree branch? Why not shoot her? True, a tree branch is easier to get rid of and much more difficult to, say, lift fingerprints from. But then why not bludgeon me the same way he'd bludgeoned Alicia? Why a gun for me and for his wife? Why not a gun for Alicia?

There was something else that was bothering me. I crept back downstairs. Despite her obvious fatigue, Aunt Ginny was at the kitchen table, bent over a thick file.

"What are you doing up?" she asked without turning to look at me.

"What are you doing, Aunt Ginny? What file is that?" I caught a glimpse of the label before she closed it and covered it with her hands. "Did you search his stuff, Aunt Ginny?"

"Whose stuff?"

"Donnelly's."

"Why do you want to know?"

"Did you find a necklace?"

"What necklace?"

"Alicia was wearing a necklace the day she died."

"Says who? I don't remember anyone saying anything about a necklace." Aunt Ginny prided herself on her memory and her ability to hold all the facts of a case in her head.

"A kid named Simon Phillips gave her a necklace. He says she was wearing it the day she died. But I don't remember seeing one when Charlie found her, and her dad said she wasn't wearing any jewelry when they went to see her, and none was returned to him." He was talking about when the Allens went to see Alicia's body. According to Ashleigh, who heard it from her mom, who went to yoga with Alicia's mother's older sister, Mr. Allen had done his best to talk his wife out of going with him to the morgue, but she'd insisted. "If she was wearing it when she died, and if it's been missing ever since, then the killer must have it. Right?"

Aunt Ginny thumbed through the papers in her file. Her frown deepened. "I don't see anything here about a necklace. I'll look into it first thing in the morning. Now go to bed."

I couldn't stop thinking about what Charlie had said. Why hadn't Donnelly just followed Alicia if he wanted to find his wife? Why kill her?

Maybe Alicia had realized she was being followed. Maybe she had confronted him. If she had, and if he'd demanded she tell, she would have refused. I was sure of it. But what if he had threatened her with a gun? Would that have made any difference?

Say Donnelly had killed her. It wasn't that much of a stretch. There was no doubt he'd been searching for his wife. And it was conceivable that he or the private detective he'd hired had stumbled onto the same thing I had—the link between Alicia and Jennifer. There was also no doubt that Donnelly was a violent man who was accustomed to using intimidation and force to get what he wanted. It wasn't hard to imagine a man like that flying into a rage when confronted by a girl who refused to tell him what he wanted to know.

But what about the necklace? Simon was sure Alicia had been wearing it the day she died. He'd even asked her parents about it at the memorial service. If Simon was right, if she'd been wearing it that day, what had happened to it? There was no mention of a necklace anywhere in Aunt Ginny's file, and I was pretty sure Alicia hadn't been wearing it when Charlie found her. So the killer must have taken it.

That's what niggled at me.

Why would Donnelly have bothered with it? To make the killing look like a robbery? If so, it hadn't worked. Or had he taken the necklace because of its value, because it was something he couldn't resist? If that was so, then it should turn up among his possessions.

There was also the unsatisfied look on Aunt Ginny's face. Something was bothering her too.

Aunt Ginny was pacing the kitchen, her cell phone pressed to her ear, when I went downstairs the next morning.

"You have to be kidding me." She glanced at me. "When? But what about—?" She frowned as she listened. "Great. Thanks for the heads-up." She tossed her phone onto the kitchen table in disgust.

"Problem?" I asked.

"The chief is holding a press conference in a couple of hours to update the media about the Alicia Allen murder."

"What kind of update?"

"Carrie's being released. Donnelly's been tagged as the murderer."

"You don't think he did it, do you, Aunt Ginny?"

"Let's just say there are a couple of loose ends remaining. And I hate loose ends." She drained her coffee cup. "I'm going in to work. Stay out of trouble, okay?"

I took my breakfast up to my room, where I read the email attachments Charlie had sent me about

Simon when Charlie had suspected him of killing Alicia. The first one was an article about a recent and prestigious international piano competition that Simon had won. A sidebar recapped the other major awards he had won, his accomplishments made all the more impressive by the tender ages at which he had won them.

A second attachment was coverage of a national competition, held in front of a live audience, which bore the headline *Pianist Melts Down Over Texting*. Apparently Simon had been distracted by the light from the phone's screen. He stopped playing, jumped down off the stage, squeezed past a dozen pairs of knees, grabbed the phone from the offender's hand and hurled it to the back of the hall, where it fell with a faint but audible *thunk*. He then jumped back onto the stage and started his piece from the beginning.

The final attachment, dated a few years back, was a profile of Simon and his mother in a magazine for parents. *Hitting the right note: What it's like to raise a child prodigy.* The article quoted his mother, a widow since Simon's toddlerhood, as saying she was not surprised by his ability *given the number of distinguished musicians in the family.* Both of his maternal grandparents, two uncles and his mother were professional musicians. She also said she wished she could get Simon outdoors more often to play like other boys his age, but that it was next to impossible to separate him from his piano.

I looked at the photos. Simon's mother had been strikingly beautiful, with a cascade of dark hair and lively brown eyes. She had been a concert pianist right up until her husband's death in an airplane crash. From then until her own death from cancer, she had dedicated herself to raising Simon. She had died four years ago.

Simon's two uncles took after their father— distinguished looking with leonine heads of hair and strong square jaws. One of them, of course, was Mr. Todd, the music teacher at our school. When I clicked on his name, I discovered that he had once been regarded as a brilliant, up-and-coming conductor. His career had ended a decade ago after psychological problems. He took up teaching.

Charlie's comment on all of this was, "This guy is weird. What if he found out Alicia didn't feel the same way about him as he felt about her? What if he found out she was interested in Brendan?"

But if Alicia had been wearing the necklace, as Simon had insisted to her parents, and if the necklace was missing precisely because the murderer had taken it, that let Simon off the hook. He'd been obviously distraught about the loss of the necklace. He wanted it back.

It wasn't hard to find out where he lived. It was a rambling Victorian farmhouse, complete with wraparound porch and gabled windows, and it stood on the outskirts of town on a full acre of land near the lift bridge. It took me nearly half an hour to get there by bike.

I heard the music—a piece for piano that sounded familiar and that I probably should have known the name of, or at least the composer. The melody flowed and blossomed until it seemed to fill the air around me. If that was Simon playing, I had to admit he sounded pretty good.

I rang the doorbell and heard its chime above the more delicate notes of the piano. The music stopped abruptly. For a moment or two I heard nothing at all, and then *whoosh*, the front door swung open and Simon's face, red and peevish, glared out at me.

"I need to talk to you, Simon," I said quickly. "It's about Alicia."

His face lost its look of annoyed impatience. He opened the door wide. "What about her?"

"Can I come in?"

He stepped aside to let me in and then closed the door behind me and waved me into the room to the left of the foyer. The music room. A grand piano on a well-lit expanse of hardwood floor. A cabinet, its door ajar just enough that I could see its contents— music. Sheets and sheets of it. Simon slid onto the piano bench.

"What about Alicia?"

I glanced around the room for somewhere to sit, but the room was empty of any other furniture except for a folding chair against one wall.

"Do you mind?" I asked.

He shrugged.

I unfolded the chair near the piano bench.

"The police chief is holding a press conference in a couple of hours. He's going to announce that they're closing her case. They know who the murderer is."

"That's not news. Carrie did it. That's what they say, right?"

I shook my head. "Not anymore. Now they're saying it was a man named Brad Donnelly."

Simon looked puzzled. "Who is he?"

I explained about Jennifer and her little boy. "Alicia was tutoring the little boy. Apparently she was good at it."

A gentle smile played across his lips. "She really liked working with kids. I can't stand them. I don't have the patience. But she loved it. She said she loved it more than anything." He paused, seemingly lost in memories. But not for long. "Did they find the necklace?"

"Not yet," I said. "Are you sure she was wearing it that day?"

"She was wearing it. She wanted to give it back to me as soon as I gave it to her, but I wouldn't take it."

"Why did she want to give it back?"

"She said because it wasn't right to take something so valuable, especially when we weren't boyfriend and girlfriend or anything like that."

"When did this happen, Simon?"

"It was the day before."

"The day before she died?"

He nodded.

"You must have been disappointed when she said that."

"I was at first. Then she told me about Brendan. She looked so happy when she talked about him. Much happier than she had been."

"Alicia was unhappy?" No one had mentioned that before. Not to me anyway.

"She missed a couple of practices with my uncle."

"She did?" This was also news to me.

"She said there was something else she had to do."

"Did she say what it was?"

He shook his head.

"What days did she have practice with your uncle?"

"Mondays and Wednesdays."

The same days she had been tutoring Teddy.

"Is that what made her unhappy? Missing practice?" I asked.

"I don't know. I don't think so. She asked me if I ever got tired of shutting myself up in a room every day after school for hours of practice." He looked at me. "I never get tired of it. But Alicia wasn't like that. I think she wanted something different."

"Did she tell you that?"

"She said that lately she felt her music was more important to everyone else than it was to her."

"Everyone else?"

"Her parents. My uncle."

All of this was interesting, but it wasn't what I'd come to ask about.

"Simon, if you told her she could keep the necklace, why did you ask her parents for it back?" I asked.

His cheeks turned as pink as the inside of a picture-book bunny's ears.

"My uncle was upset that I gave it to her. My mother left it to me. I thought I could do whatever I wanted with it. But my uncle said no. He said it had been in the family for four generations and that I was supposed to give it to my wife when I got married, and then it's supposed to go to my daughter, if I have one, or to my oldest son if I don't have a daughter."

"Is it valuable?"

"If you mean is it worth a lot of money, not exactly. I mean, it's not worthless. I'm sure it's worth something.

But mostly I think it's the sentimental value. I think that's why my uncle was upset."

"Did the Allens return it to you?"

"They said they didn't have it."

Still that niggling question. Where was the necklace?

The front door opened. Simon and I both turned at the same time.

"Why isn't this door locked? Simon, haven't I told you—"

Mr. Todd appeared in the foyer, four bulging plastic shopping bags hanging from one hand, his keys dangling from his left hand. He stopped in mid-turn and mid-sentence when he saw me.

"Ms. Donovan, isn't it? What brings you here? I didn't realize you and Simon knew each other."

"She came to give me some news," Simon said.

Mr. Todd set the bags of groceries on a small table beside the stairs so that he could pocket his keys and remove his jacket. "What news?"

I stood up. "I should leave and let you practice," I said to Simon. An idea was taking shape in my head, and I wanted to talk to Aunt Ginny.

"Simon?" Mr. Todd started to gather his shopping bags to take to the kitchen. "What news?"

"About Alicia."

Mr. Todd looked at me with interest. "What about her?"

Simon answered. "They're saying it was a man who killed Alicia."

"A man?" Mr. Todd paused for a second, two shopping bags in one hand, one in the other. "But I thought—"

"That it was Carrie. So did I. Everyone did."

Mr. Todd reached for the last bag. "I'm afraid I don't understand."

"They're going to let Carrie go. They don't think she did it."

"Lovely," Mr. Todd said, in a tone that signified lack of interest more than it did an appreciation of justice. "You need to get back to practicing, Simon. I'll show your visitor out."

He stood aside slightly, making way for me to move from the music room to the foyer.

"When are you going to tell Carrie?" Simon asked.

"Tell her what?"

"That she's going to be in the youth orchestra."

"Good God, Simon, whatever gave you that idea?" his uncle asked.

"She told you that's what she wanted."

"Yes, well, you of all people should know we don't always get what we want." Mr. Todd nodded impatiently at the door. "If you wouldn't mind, Ms. Donovan, Simon and I both have work to do."

I looked back at Simon. "That's what who wanted?" I asked.

"Alicia. She said my uncle should give Carrie the spot."

"Really, Simon, where did you get such a ridiculous idea?" Mr. Todd said.

Simon drew back at the rebuke. His shoulders slumped, marring his perfect piano posture.

"When did she tell you that, Simon?" I asked gently.

Simon raised his head. "The last time she was here."

Mr. Todd sighed and shook his head and set down his bags of groceries. He took me by the arm and nudged me out of the music room and into the foyer. "Simon was very fond of Alicia. But I suppose you know that already."

Simon persisted. "She asked you, Uncle Richard. She asked you to make sure Carrie got her spot in the orchestra. She said Carrie deserved it. I heard her."

If that made any impression on Mr. Todd, I didn't see it. "If you'll come with me."

It wasn't a question, and he was through nudging. He pushed me.

"When did she say that, Simon?" I asked.

"Simon is mistaken, Ms. Donovan. Now I really must insist." He clamped a hand around my upper arm to stop me from going back to Simon.

"The last time she was here," Simon said. "Wednesday. She showed up in time for practice, but she didn't stay. You had that big argument with her. Remember, Uncle Richard?"

My mind raced. If what Simon said was true, Alicia had been tiring of music and had turned her attention elsewhere. She had missed at least one practice and had blown off another on the day she died, which was also a day she had been expected at Jennifer's to tutor Teddy. She had never shown up there. I wondered about the youth-orchestra bombshell Simon had just dropped. Alicia didn't want the position. Carrie was next in line. But as far as

I knew, no one had ever told her that. Instead, she had ended up the prime suspect in Alicia's murder. The threatening note found in the music room had pretty much sealed her fate until Brad Donnelly showed up looking for his wife. Carrie admitted to having written the note, but insisted she didn't mean it. She had passed it to Tina, and I'd thought Tina had used it to point the finger of blame at Carrie. But what if it hadn't been Tina? What if it had been someone else? What if it had been someone with almost limitless access to the music room?

I knew Mr. Todd had spoken to the police. Apparently he told them that nothing had seemed out of the ordinary with Alicia. He hadn't mentioned the missed practices or the argument he had had with her. Nor had he said anything about Alicia bowing out of the national youth orchestra or her wish that Carrie be given her spot.

And the missing necklace? The person who valued it the most was Mr. Todd. Simon had been happy to give it to Alicia as a symbol of their friendship. Mr. Todd was upset that he had gifted it outside of the family. If Mr. Todd had killed Alicia, he could have taken back the necklace.

But even if that were true, it still left a huge question: Why? What possible motive did Mr. Todd have for killing her?

"Your uncle is right, Simon. I should get out of here and let you practice."

I needed to call Aunt Ginny. She needed to know everything I had found out. Maybe she could use the information to get a search warrant for the necklace.

Mr. Todd still had me by the arm, but he was no longer trying to get me out the door. He was holding me back.

"Simon, go to your room."

Simon balked at the order. "You just told me to practice."

"Now I'm telling you to go to your room. This minute." His hand was biting deep into my upper arm.

"Don't go, Simon," I said. I didn't want to be alone with Mr. Todd. I needed Simon, and I needed him on my side.

"To your room," his uncle boomed. "Now."

"You were here the day Alicia was murdered, weren't you, Simon?"

"Simon, are you defying me?"

"You were here, Simon," I continued. "You heard Alicia talking to your uncle. You heard them arguing. What happened after Alicia left, Simon? Did your uncle stay in the house, or did he go out?"

Simon's brow furrowed as he thought back to that day.

"He went out," he said. "He was angry. He grabbed his keys and went out."

"Did he say where he went?"

Simon shook his head.

"Why don't you ask him now, Simon? Ask your uncle where he went after Alicia left the house."

"For the last time, go to your room, Simon, or face the consequences."

"I have a better idea, Simon," I said. "Come with me. Tell the police everything you just told me. You want to make sure they find Alicia's murderer, don't you?"

"What rubbish. Simon, if I have to tell you one more time, you're grounded."

"Come on, Simon."

Simon hesitated. He frowned at his uncle. Then he came toward us. "Okay," he said.

Mr. Todd spun me around so that his back was against the door and I was between him and Simon.

"I'm afraid I can't let you leave just yet."

"Why not?" Simon asked.

"What are you going to do, Mr. Todd? You can't keep me here indefinitely. And Simon is involved now."

That's when someone rang the doorbell.

Mr. Todd clamped a hand over my mouth. "Go to your room, Simon," he hissed.

The doorbell rang again, followed by brisk knocking.

"Police!"

Aunt Ginny.

I lifted one foot and stomped down as hard as I could on the bridge of Mr. Todd's foot. He released his grip on me, and I shouted.

"Aunt Ginny, help!"

"Riley?" The doorknob rattled, but the door was locked.

Mr. Todd pushed me away from the door, but I ducked under his arms and unlocked the door. Aunt Ginny stood framed in the doorway. She had her gun drawn. It was trained on Mr. Todd.

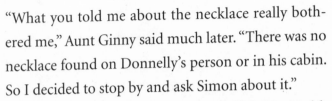

"What you told me about the necklace really bothered me," Aunt Ginny said much later. "There was no necklace found on Donnelly's person or in his cabin. So I decided to stop by and ask Simon about it."

This was after she had handcuffed Mr. Todd, and after Simon had slowly put the pieces together and realized what his uncle was being accused of. Then two uniformed officers showed up, which was perfect timing, because Simon flew at his uncle and started pummeling him. For a slight guy, he had the strength of a lion. It took both uniforms to separate uncle and nephew. Another squad car showed up. Todd, still handcuffed, was bundled into the back of one. Simon, an important witness, went into another to be taken to the station for questioning. I rode back with Aunt Ginny. As we were leaving, two more cops were pulling on latex gloves in preparation for searching the house.

When we got back to the police station, Aunt Ginny installed me in the coffee room. She had no choice. Simon and Mr. Todd were occupying the only two interview rooms. She was pouring herself a cup of coffee when her cell phone rang. She listened and fist-pumped the air. She was smiling when she hung up.

"Did they find the necklace?" I asked.

Aunt Ginny nodded. "He hid it—at the bottom of a box of cereal."

"They even searched his food?"

"Yup. Officer Pulaski found it."

"Wow, is he ever thorough."

"Actually, it was an accident," Aunt Ginny said. "And a breach of protocol. He's being disciplined."

"I don't get it. What did he do wrong?"

"He was assigned to search the kitchen. Apparently the suspect had several boxes of a certain luxury imported chocolate biscuit from Austria, one of which was opened. Josh literally caught Officer Pulaski with his hand in the cookie jar. Pulaski tried to act as if he hadn't done anything wrong. In the process, he knocked over some boxes, including an opened box of cereal, and *voilà!* You know what that means, right?"

"It means Donnelly didn't kill Alicia. Mr. Todd did."

"It means that the chief was wrong." She was still smiling when she told me to sit tight while she went to question Mr. Todd.

I'd left the house in the morning to ask Simon about the necklace. It was after midnight by the time Aunt Ginny and I were in her car and on our way home. By then Mr. Todd had been charged.

"He's pleading not guilty," Aunt Ginny told me.

"But he did it. You know he did."

"Apparently Todd has a history of instability. He assaulted one of his students when she got pregnant and wanted to stay home with her baby instead of continuing with her music career. It was hushed up and settled out of court by the conservatory where he worked. I think his lawyer is planning to use that to argue he wasn't criminally responsible."

"Is that why he killed Alicia? Because she didn't want to join the youth orchestra?"

"He says she threw her life away. He seems to think she could have been world-class. He couldn't understand why she would just blow it off. He says he tried to reason with her, but she wouldn't listen. He says he doesn't even remember hitting her."

"How is Simon taking it?"

Aunt Ginny glanced at me. "He's an odd duck."

"He's a musical prodigy," I said. "So was his mother. But otherwise he's just a kid. He had a massive crush on Alicia. Is he going to be okay?"

"There's another uncle," Aunt Ginny said. "He's been contacted."

"And Donnelly's wife?"

"She's relieved. She finally gets her life back."

"And Rafe?"

"He saved your life. He's in the clear."

Our house came into view in the beam of the headlights.

"I'm starving," Aunt Ginny said. "Do we have anything to eat?"

They released Carrie. She turned up at my house a few days later.

"I just wanted to thank you," she said. She was paler than the last time I had seen her and had lost a lot of weight. "You were the only person who believed me."

"Desiree believed you too," I told her. "She's a good friend. She told me she wanted to visit you, but your parents refused to put her name on the approved-visitor list."

At the mention of her parents, Carrie bowed her head.

"I don't know what I'm going to do," she said softly. "I know they thought I did it. Marion in particular. She told me she was sorry, but I don't think she is. I think she's still angry that I made her look bad."

"Maybe she'll see things differently now."

She shook her head.

"I'm not going to live there anymore. I talked to a social worker before I was released. I can get some financial aid so that I can support myself until the end of the school year. I'm moving too. I found a room for rent. I don't want to live here anymore, not after what happened."

What she really meant was not after what people believed she had done. I understood how she must have been feeling. But I wasn't sure that moving was the best solution. Still, people do what they feel they have to do, and maybe it would turn out to be a good thing for her. Maybe she needed a fresh start.

"Have you talked to Tina?" I asked.

"Not yet."

"Are you going to?"

"I don't know. I'm not blaming her for what happened. But I know she didn't stick up for me. And if anyone should have, it should have been her."

"Some people need more time to figure things out." I believed it when I said it, but I also knew it sounded pretty lame to Carrie after everything she'd been through.

"Maybe. It doesn't matter. What matters is that you believed me. If it wasn't for you, I'd probably still be under arrest."

"I hope things work out for you," I told Carrie.

She hugged me briefly and stepped out into the night.

AN EXCERPT FROM

FROM ABOVE

NORAH McCLINTOCK

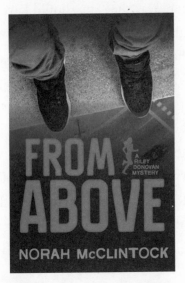

978-1-4598-0933-8 $10.95 pb

ONE

A damp, dreary day was made drearier by Ashleigh's lateness. Where was she? She should have been here ages ago. I glanced at the clock on the wall. Okay, she should have been here five minutes ago. But it wasn't as if this was some last-minute thing she might have forgotten. She had been meeting me every day after class since school began. We did our homework together on the days she wasn't working. I walked her to the grocery store on the days she was. That meant I never had to walk past Mike Winters' locker alone.

Mike's locker was the first one at the top of the stairs. He was always there after school, and it took him forever to get his stuff together. I'd never seen a guy take so long. It meant that I couldn't leave—okay, so I *refused* to leave—okay, okay, so I was *afraid* to leave—without having someone like Ashleigh leave with me. I realize how that makes me sound. But it's the truth.

Get over it, I told myself. What had happened, happened. It was history now. Besides, everything had turned out okay, hadn't it? Sure, I'd accused Mike of terrible things. But I'd done it in good faith. I'd believed what I said at the time that I said it. It might be a lame defense, but it's also the truth.

"Boo!"

I jumped and spun around, my heart pounding. Ashleigh.

"Are you still here?" She seemed surprised.

"Of course I'm still here. I was waiting for you. Remember?"

"In that case, you're lucky I came this way." When she saw the blank look on my face, she shook her head. "You forgot, didn't you?"

"*Me*? You're the one who forgot. We meet here at the same time every day."

"Except for today. I told you, Riley. It's picture day."

"What?" Picture day? Today? "When? Now?"

Ashleigh was right. I had forgotten. Otherwise I would have paid more attention to my hair. I would have dressed differently. There was no way I wanted to appear in my first-ever school yearbook with a greasy mop of hair and a pilled sweater that was the first warm thing I'd grabbed this morning. I blamed Mr. Jespers. If he hadn't given us a ridiculous assignment—a multimedia presentation that expressed our individuality—I wouldn't have stayed up half the night editing old videos together with music that was important to me. I would have gotten up in time to attend to my personal hygiene. I rooted in my backpack for my brush and wished I'd stuck a mirror to the inside of my locker the way most of the other girls had done.

And I cursed school. I'd never liked the idea of it. I definitely did not enjoy the practice of it. When I'd lived with my grandpa Jimmy, which I had for most of my life, school had consisted of distance education via computer. That's because Jimmy had been constantly on the road with his rock group, which had had half a dozen hit songs before I was born. When Jimmy died, I had been shipped off to live with Aunt Ginny, my mother's younger sister. Her father, my grandpa Dan, took over my education for a while. But a couple of months back, Aunt Ginny had been offered a plum job, and we'd moved to Moorebridge. Result: I was forced to enrol in school.

"Relax," Ashleigh said. "It's not *that* picture day. It's National Student Photography Day. Hey, what happened to your four-leaf clover?"

"What?" I looked at the small fabric loop on my backpack where the green-and-gold clover had hung ever since Charlie had given it to me for my fifteenth birthday. *So your year will be filled with good luck*, he'd said. But the clover was gone. I scanned the floor frantically.

"Maybe it fell off in your locker," Ashleigh said.

I searched it thoroughly. The clover wasn't there.

"It could be anywhere." I moaned. "I don't even know how long it's been missing."

"I'd help you look, but like I said, it's—"

"—National Student Photography Day. What is that anyway?"

"You didn't listen to me at all, did you?" She let

out a dramatic sigh and rattled off a description that I had to admit sounded vaguely familiar. "It's a contest. Students right across the country participate. There's a theme every year. And the rule is that everyone has to take their picture on the same day at the same time—no cheating. There are great prizes—cash and cameras."

"And you're participating?" It was amazing how much I didn't know about my best friend. I'd had no idea at all that Ashleigh was interested in photography. In my defense, Ashleigh and I had met a mere two months ago, when I moved here with Aunt Ginny.

"You bet I am. I came fourth in the regionals last year. I won a great camera." She dug in her backpack and produced it. "Digital, but professional quality." She glanced at the clock above the bank of lockers. "I really have to go. We only have two hours to get the perfect shot."

"What's the theme?"

"From above."

"From above what?"

She grinned. "From above whatever you decide. One guy I know ditched his afternoon classes so he can be on the top of Bald Mountain in time to try to get a shot of the eagle's nest up there."

"There are eagles on Bald Mountain?" That was news to me.

"One girl is going to photograph lake life from the surface. You know, from above."

"That'll be fun in the rain," I said. It had started drizzling while I was riding to school. The drizzle had turned into a downpour, which had eventually slowed to a steady shower that continued all day. I wasn't looking forward to the wet ride home.

"Look out a window," Ashleigh said. "The rain stopped fifteen minutes ago. The sun is out. And FYI, Mike pulled some strings with one of his uncles to get permission to go up on the water tower and get some panorama shots that he wants to turn into one picture of the whole town."

"Mike *Winters?*" The same Mike whose cutting glances I had been dodging for weeks? "Mike Winters competes in photography contests?"

"I know he doesn't seem like the type. But he's good," Ashleigh said. "You wouldn't ever guess it, because he can be such a jerk. But put a camera in his hands and he's a different person. He has an eye for a great shot. I heard him tell someone else in the camera club that he likes the way things look through a lens."

"What does that mean?"

"I have no idea. But wait till you see my entry." She stowed her camera in her pack. "Gotta run." She raced down the hall, leaving me to contemplate the notion of Mike Winters' artistic eye. She was right. I never would have guessed.

I rolled up my rain poncho, stuffed it in my backpack and went boldly down the stairs and out the front door.

My bike was locked up at the recreation center next door to Lyle Murcheson Regional High School. Unlike the school, the rec center had proper bike stands. On my way there, I scanned every square inch of wet and puddled ground, hoping to spot something twinkling in the afternoon sun. Something like, say, a green-and-gold four-leaf clover. But the only sparkling items I saw were wadded-up gum wrappers and a nickel. I had to find that charm. Charlie was already mad at me for something that wasn't my fault. Now he was going to think I'd ditched his gift on purpose.

I didn't find Charlie's clover in the schoolyard, so I kept my eyes on the ground as I walked slowly behind the almost-brand-new rec center, praying that I'd find the charm before I reached the bike stands. Then I heard what can only be called a blood-curdling scream.

The scream was followed almost instantly by a chorus of other, higher-pitched shrieks. At first I thought it was from some ridiculous girl drama. You wouldn't believe what the girls at my school screech about—everything from a new episode of their favorite TV show to the release of a movie starring the newest, hottest actor. It was pathetic. So when I heard all that yowling, I rolled my eyes.

Until someone shrieked, "Call an ambulance!"

Ambulance equals serious. I ran toward the commotion and found a clutch of girls in cheerleader uniforms, which explained the girly squealing. No one screams louder than a cheerleader. Put a squad of them together, and it's hyper-banshee time. These cheerleaders were huddled on the pavement behind the rec center, where, I guess, they had decided to practice, given the squishiness of the school athletic field.

But the squad wasn't practising fan-thrilling cheers. Most of them weren't even moving. Instead, they were frozen to the spot and staring at the ground. At something *on* the ground. Correction. At some*one*. I saw his—judging from the size of the shoes— sneakered feet first. The toes pointed to two o'clock and ten o'clock. I couldn't see his face right away, but from the way some girls were crying and others were moaning *ohmygawd, ohmygawd, ohmygawd*, it was clear not only that something bad had happened but also that they knew the person to whom it had happened.

The nearest cheerleader must have sensed an outsider, because she turned to me and clutched my arm. "Do you have a phone?"

I reached around to the side pocket of my backpack, extracted my cell phone and elbowed my way to the front of the cluster of girls. I wished I hadn't.

Ethan Crawford, one of Lyle High's standout athletes, was spread-eagle face up on the pavement, his thickly lashed hazel eyes staring up at where the breaking clouds were shifting slowly across the sky. He didn't blink. He couldn't. He wasn't breathing.

How could he, with all that blood pooled on the ground under his head?

I punched 9-1-1 into my phone. While I waited for an answer, I looked up. Where Ethan was lying—not far from the base of a wall, feet closest to the wall, head farthest from it—as well as how he was lying—on his back, arms and legs outstretched—made me think he had fallen from above. I looked up. The sun chose that moment to break through the thinning cloud. It blinded me, and I raised a hand to shield my eyes. When I did, I caught a glimpse of someone on the roof of the rec center. At least, I *thought* that was what it was. A head and shoulders. A cheerleader grabbed my arm.

"Ambulance!" she screamed. "He needs an ambulance."

I looked up again. Whoever had been there was gone.

NORAH McCLINTOCK won the Crime Writers of Canada's Arthur Ellis Award for crime fiction for young people five times. She wrote more than sixty YA novels, including two other Riley Donovan books, and contributed to the Seven Prequels, Seven (the series), the Seven Sequels and the Secrets series.